SOMETHING I'M NOT

Something I'm Not

LUCY BERESFORD

Duckworth Overlook

First published in 2008 by
Duckworth Overlook
90-93 Cowcross Street, London EC1M 6BF
Tel: 020 7490 7300
Fax: 020 7490 0080
info@duckworth-publishers.co.uk
www.ducknet.co.uk

A catalogue record for this book is available
from the British Library

ISBN 978-0-7156-3709-8

Typeset by Ray Davies
Printed and bound in Great Britain by
Cromwell Press, Trowbridge, Wilts

This book is for Guy,

my eternal flame

We tend to be incredibly distrustful of our own perceptions ...
we do not trust ourselves as witnesses ...
and ultimately we surrender and give ourselves over
to a process of perpetual interpretation,
applied even to those things we know to be absolute fact ...

— JAVIER MARÍAS, *Your Face Tomorrow*,
1: Fever and Spear

Prologue

'I DON'T KNOW if you ever catch Robbie Taylor,' says Amber, by way of avoiding Dr Ramji's question. 'We had him on in the car coming here. He runs a sort of therapy phone-in. Not sure I'd broadcast the secrets of my psyche to an audience of millions—'

Amber hesitates. The woman in the opposite armchair sits absolutely still. Amber wants to continue, but she is distracted by the woman's eyebrows, immaculate crescents of smooth, dark hairs along the line of the brow. Anger flutters at Amber's throat, and she wants to shake the woman. Is it jealousy, in the face of such perfection? Shame, at being caught skirting the issue with therapy small talk? Or a fear that Dr Ramji knows all?

'—so it took a radio show to make me see that, actually, I'm very lucky.' Strident is how Amber hears herself sound.

'Lucky,' says Dr Ramji, her voice a warm drink on a cold night. She cocks her head in a way Amber bets she has to practise. 'In what sense?'

'Well, my husband says—'

'Matthys?'

Panic prickles Amber's skin, as if this woman's correct pronunciation of Matt's Afrikaans name has somehow upped the stakes in a hitherto covert competition. Amber glances round the room, with its surfaces free from paperwork, before noticing a pinboard on the wall. It is covered with a collage: various Madonna and child postcards, and Polaroids of newborn babies. Amber's stomach churns, and she refocuses on the doctor.

'Where was I? Oh yes, Matt. Well, he's a psychiatrist. He works with people at their wits' end. I guess you get them like that here, too.' The doctor makes no comment. 'Which makes me realise that the life I've created is good.'

'So it's been a conscious process,' says Dr Ramji.

Amber feels the words brush against her skin. She senses the minute movements of air between the doctor and herself. Always there are hidden meanings in a woman's speech. Again she glances at the pinboard, her eye drawn to a postcard by Joshua Reynolds. It's of a girl hugging a puppy. And, maybe it's her imagination, but in the room she now catches a warm scent of incense.

'There was a letter.' Again the doctor remains silent, and Amber feels tears welling up in her eyes. 'I was five or six. My school was perched on the shingle bank beside a bird sanctuary. The school rented the building from the sanctuary, and most days we had nature study. Brent geese flew in from Russia, and we plotted their route on a map in the classroom. Sometimes we got to hold newborn chicks, their warm bodies flickering in our hands.' Amber looks up. 'I'm sure you don't want to hear this—'

Amber notices the doctor tuck stray hairs of her geometric cut behind one ear. It's a simple gesture that makes Dr Ramji suddenly seem very competent, very containing. Amber can whisper secrets, tell her anything, and Dr Ramji will make sense of it all.

'There was a letter.' Amber clears her throat. 'To parents. From my teacher, Miss Gibson. Announcing the arrival of baby field mice, and future plans to loan them out at weekends. To *responsible* children. A sort of rodent sleepover. The letter was to get parental permission. I ran all the way home that afternoon, to make sure my mother got it as quickly as possible.' Amber stares into her lap.

'The next morning, over porridge, I watched my mother sign the form and slide it into a used envelope. At registration, Miss Gibson collected the forms (mine was the only one in an envelope) and announced that on Thursday she'd post a rota on the noticeboard—'

Amber cannot sit still. The Reynolds painting keeps catching her eye. The girl's cheeks are flushed with pleasure as she squeezes the puppy on her lap. Amber has not recalled the episode of the mice for thirty years. And yet, it's as though something inside Amber has lately cut loose. The letter to Miss Gibson is now as vivid as this evening's drive through the November drizzle to Dr Ramji's clinic.

All week, she's imagined the mice (christened Hector, Kiki and Zaza) in her home. It's like waiting for Christmas. And she wants so badly to see her place on the rota she decides to set off for school earlier than usual. She can feel her heart pumping.

The Reynolds girl, clutching her pet, gazes down at Amber. Amber blinks away.

'I stood in front of the noticeboard for ages. I knew how to spell my name, and the names of all my friends, even long ones like Stephanie's, because I went to her birthday party, and wrote in her card. But where was my name? Its capital *A*? Why wasn't I on the list?

'I turned at the sound of Miss Gibson walking towards me. I used to think the tap of her heels in the corridors was like a white stick on a pavement. "What are you doing here so early, Amber?" she said to me. "I didn't expect to see you reading this list." She looked confused. My eyes filled, blurring her. I wanted to say that she'd forgotten my name, but the idea in my head was too jumbled up.

'"I am sorry your name won't be on the list, Amber," Miss Gibson said. "You should have told us the truth." Her eyes narrowed on me. "You might have become seriously ill. Thank goodness your mother saw fit to inform me that you are highly allergic to animal fur."'

Amber reaches into her handbag and retrieves a tissue. Dabbing her eyes, she notices a pair of unfamiliar ankles, elegant, precisely crossed, and remembers where she is. She looks up and tries to smile at Dr Ramji. 'I'm sorry. I'm not sure where all that came from.' She blows her nose, and tucks the tissue up her sleeve.

'What did Miss Gibson say when you told her the truth?' asks Dr Ramji, in an even voice.

'When I told her?' cries Amber, fresh tears sliding down her cheeks. 'What could I say? That it was my mother who dislikes helpless creatures? I overheard her at coffee mornings, saying she didn't really like children. Although all mothers love their own. Don't they?'

Dr Ramji leans forward in her chair. 'You don't seem so sure.'

Amber's gaze darts once more to the Reynolds girl before settling on the doctor's groomed brows. 'My friends are my family now,' Amber whispers.

'In what sense?'

Amber flicks an imaginary thread from her trousers. 'It's complicated.'

'You know you can take—?'

'—my time. Yes, but everyone's waiting downstairs. Shouldn't we just get on with the surgery?'

'They can wait,' says the doctor emphatically, reaching out across her polished coffee table to activate an answer machine.

And, as the doctor settles back in her armchair, Amber finds herself taking a deep breath and exhaling slowly before starting to speak.

Chapter One

I'M THE kind of person who plans my spontaneity. Matt's not on call this weekend and, apart from some CVs I've brought home, our weekend is free. Which means a structure is in place.

The CVs should only take a couple of hours; those that mention long gaps in employment and a large family to support are the hardest to read. Then, while I'm preparing supper, I'll watch a video of last month's men's Wimbledon final; it's how I like my sport, knowing from the start who'll win. Supper is for catching up with my oldest friend, Dylan. Or, rather, meeting his new boyfriend.

The heat this summer has been relentless. Strangers complain to one another of discomfort. London Underground's schedules have disintegrated, and, with them, commuters' patience. Weather forecasters sound increasingly apologetic, as if they know their bulletins to be morally reprehensible. A vicar in South Wales declares the hellish temperatures to be a sign of God's wrath over America's homosexual bishop. And it seems to me that the known world is suffocating, and that this will be averted only when hand-knitted ghosts from our past are cast off.

And I'm reminded of Dad, currently snoozing upstairs. He and his friend Audrey are staying the weekend. This morning we went to what he calls the Stately Tate, meaning the old one. Escaped the heat by entering its coolness. I watched as, at eighty, he hurried down the corridor the way a mother might bustle into the kitchen to fetch treats. You'd never guess he'd had a minor stroke earlier this year. By the time Audrey and I, in our leisurely gossip, had finally caught up with him, my dad the erstwhile potter was busy studying the ceramics made by a well-known transvestite. Classical-shaped vases evoking genteel sensibilities, yet decorated with disturbing images and text. 'Wonderful,' my father wheezed, tears in his eyes. 'Just exquisite.'

I wasn't sure quite what to say. Did I really want Dad seeing pictures of abused children, or reading slogans about paedophiles? Did he even know they were there? Or was his approval, one artist to another, misconceived? I tried to lead him away.

He laughed. 'If a tranny potter from Essex can find ways in this world to be comfortable in his own skin, Amber darling, then so can you!' And his bony hands had patted mine.

I warned him years ago that Matt and I won't be providing him with grandchildren. I don't think I've ever wanted to be a mother. Not even when I was little was I drawn to dolls or small animals like my friends were; some took home the class mice for the weekend, but I was never interested. And, in any case, my mother told me that girls who played with dolls that wet themselves were common.

As a teenager reading *Jackie* (when my mother hadn't confiscated it), I fantasised about marrying the perfect boy, but never pushing a pram. Boyfriends came and went. Some of them I slept with. I asked none of them, in that dreamy post-coital haze, how many children they wanted. My last boyfriend was Matt.

Matt had been at school with Dylan. And I am for ever in Dylan's debt for fixing us up. Matt is tall and sandy-haired, his skin a flush of beautiful freckles. When we first met, he reminded me of an antelope, his athleticism exuding the good health of a childhood spent on an orange farm. I often imagine him as a boy, with skinny bronzed limbs, and always with a ball of some description in his hands. And somewhere deep down I think that, in marrying him, I hoped to marry into a childhood of vast, blue skies and ripe fruit.

But first, of course, I had to have That Conversation. The one about having children. And, having fallen in love practically at first sight, I decided on full disclosure after we'd been dating only a fortnight. Better, I figured, to know up front than to torture myself for months or maybe years, and get it wrong. And so I cooked him *coq au vin*, and after a few beers, and wearing the white jeans Matt had told me made my bottom look peachy (I am nothing if not thorough), I confessed to a dormant maternal instinct. And Matt had covered my hands in his own and replied that he'd always felt ambivalent about children, and that in his view one needed to be very passionate indeed about the prospect of creating life. He had gone on to add that if he were to marry a woman desperate for children, he'd probably go on to be the father of a rugby team. But that that wouldn't happen, because he wanted to marry *me*.

Part of me was shocked by the speed of this declaration, how it propelled us to a new land I hadn't realised I longed to visit. And part of me felt relieved that finally I'd been found.

I turn my mind to the impending dinner party. That sweltering summer afternoon, I assemble ingredients. A childhood dazzled by Fanny Cradock and the *Galloping Gourmet* has fostered in me an addiction to *mise en place*. Dylan claims that I count out salt grains; that my food preparation is an art form which makes Shock and Awe look positively slipshod. I just like following recipes.

I throw scrag ends of leek into the bin and lean against the jamb of the French doors. I inhale the scent of parched soil, and watch Matt tidying the borders of our London garden. He calls it a window box on steroids. In our marital ecosystem, Matt is head gardener, my glossy-haired Mellors. Watching him do practical things makes my arms tingle. His tongue peeps out when he does manual tasks. Weeding, he has his back to me, its broad sweep lightly brown. Matt only has to stick his head out the window to tan a mellow shade of butterscotch. I want to go to him and place a kiss on his neck, to drink of his sweetness. Just then Matt turns and, leaning into the trowel, displays one of his warm smiles. These never fail to delight me, for when Matt smiles grooves appear on either side of his mouth, elegant punctuation marks drawing attention to something significant. From the moment Dylan introduced us, I was aware of Matt's enviable warm spirit; with smiles so benevolent, they appeared to offer redemption.

'What time are we expecting the Pol Roger Padre?' Matt grins.

'The usual – the minute you uncork the wine!'

The last of the sun grazes the top of the garden wall. Its colour reminds me of the carrot purée I've made in case Dylan's on one of his short-lived food-elimination regimes.

'Everything in the kitchen under control?' Matt asks, getting up. His right knee creaks.

'Of course,' I say.

'Dad and Audrey having their siesta?'

I grin. 'Yes.'

'Only, I was thinking of getting out of these,' he pulls off his gardening gloves, 'and having a quick shower.' He wears that smile which is like chewing toffee.

I lead him inside.

Chapter Two

DYLAN AND DAVID arrive for supper with two cats – the unnamed runts of a litter dropped by David's daughter's pet. It takes me a while to get my head around all this, but what with a risotto, the purée, a jar of Audrey's home-made chutney and a ripe Epoisse which I can't eat but whose ribald smell is sufficient compensation, there is ample time to hear the story of what Dylan calls David's 'road to Damascus'.

And, as David describes how he'd always suspected he was homosexual (enunciating all five vowel sounds, clearly relishing saying the word aloud), and how marriage to flame-haired Caryl only reinforced his suspicions, I find myself thinking about how our lives are changed by the choices we make, and how brave you'd have to be to have a change of heart.

Like my dad leaving my mother. I watch him help Audrey to some cheese, his gnarled hand firm on the knife, the blue veins standing proud from the pressure. I can almost feel his potter's grip from when he used to wrap me in a towel at bathtime. I collect the pudding bowls from the cupboard and, as I set them down, see that he and Audrey are holding hands under the table.

*

Somehow, we end up keeping the cats. David intended them as child substitutes for his broody lover, and brought them to dinner *en route* to staying the night at what Dylan likes to call, with no little irony, his vicar-cage. After coffee, and having been banned from doing the washing up, Dad and Audrey have gone to bed. Dylan sits at the grand piano: a present from Matt to me when he was made a consultant. Its glossy lid is home to framed photos – two dozen or more: our wedding, a skiing trip, parties, christenings. I have my hair up. I have a bob. I have stick-on flicks. I have a henna rinse. I am blonde. I'm with friends; I'm holding their babies. Matt is kissing me.

Dylan is playing the piano. A female ball of fur and bones has commandeered his lap. Dylan is running through the songs to a Stephen Sondheim musical he hopes to stage to raise money to repair his church roof. His mother, Pamela, is threatening to audition. The male cat jumps off David's knees, and saunters into a piano leg.

'That cat's got Amber's sense of direction!' guffaws Matt.

'Better that', I snap, 'than that he has your sense of humour.' Matt rises to close the front shutters and plants a noisy kiss on my head as he passes.

'You guys!' says David, whose hair reminds me of a startled grey mammal. I watch him flick cat fur from his combat trousers. *Let's hope it doesn't fly up and get caught in the braces on his teeth*. When I stop my silent bitch-fest, I realise that Dylan has been making up a song about the cats, which he has christened Tim and Tallulah.

'Keep them!' cries Dylan, thudding a final chord before swivelling round on the stool.

'Now I know how Mary must have felt before the Angel Gabriel,' says Matt, solemnly.

My insides curdle. *Has Matt changed his mind about having children?* 'Don't be daft, Dylan,' I say quickly.

'Why not? I'm running a retreat in a couple of days' time, so, as much as David wants me to have them—'

'Don't be daft,' I repeat, buying time for Matt to ride to my rescue, slay this evil offer and keep our pairing intact. As a psychiatrist, he's rigid on boundaries. Apparently patients hate his professional neutrality, and attempt all manner of personal intrusions. They quiz him, wanting him as their special friend, their surrogate parent. And Matt smiles (at least I always picture him in his office smiling, since he's always smiling at me), and scribbles a note or two on a pad. Then he wonders aloud why they want to know. This annoys them intensely, which makes for more notes, more smiles.

'Sounds like a great idea,' says Matt.

I glare at my husband. 'Are they house-trained?' I ask, as if remotely interested.

'They're barely five weeks old.'

'Dylan tells me you've decided not to have kids—' I note the way David slips this in, as if to say, *Dylan's told me everything about you* '—so you won't have to worry about small hands accidentally shutting them in the washing machine.'

'It's not *their* welfare I'm worried about,' I snap.

'And they do so match your Farrow & Ball paintwork,' he adds, raising an eyebrow. I meet his look with one of my own, as a nickname for him, 'Camp David', takes up residence in my head.

Matt is on his haunches by the fireplace. One kitten is on its hind legs, tugging with its front paws at Matt's sleeve; the other is being tickled, eyes half-closed in apparent ecstasy. A parent playing with the children. I feel a sharp stitch in my left side. 'Dyl, why me?'

'Because we're like family, you and me. Friends are the new family—'

'Like white is the new black,' smirks David. I want to slug him.

'And they're sooooo adorable,' says Dylan, watching Matt and the cats.

'So, *you* have them, Dyl—' Then I stop, realising in that moment that all three men are now looking at me in a particularly complicit way. My chest feels tight. I rub my collarbone.

'All right,' I say with a sigh. 'But only until you're back from your retreat.' I watch as Matt rises to close the French windows. 'Then you must have them. You're the broody one around here.'

David taps his watch and reminds Dylan of his eight o'clock Communion tomorrow morning. He goes out to his car and returns with a cardboard box, which contains all the paraphernalia novice parents of juvenile cats need for those crucial first nights at home. Dylan is hunching on his jacket. Watching him flick his Pre-Raphaelite curls out from under the collar, a sudden rush of feeling floods my body. His eyes are red and watery, as if leaving the cats behind constitutes a loss of insurmountable proportions.

There is a pause. David, hovering by the car, clears his throat. I have this fleeting sense, perhaps incorrect, that David is prompting Dylan, that he's taking control.

Dylan looks at me again, and this time his squeeze at the tops of my arms is just a little too sharp. 'Darling, I meant to tell you earlier. David and I, we're thinking of adopting.'

Chapter Three

I AM STANDING in bare feet, gripping the basin in one hand. With the other I pull at strands of blonde hair along my parting – I do not need to use the bathroom mirror in front of me. My fingers detect subtle textural differences, dropping those that feel too smooth, too regular, gently tugging until one strand remains between thumb and middle finger, a strand slightly thicker than all the rest, and therefore from experience more likely to be a darker shade, a strand punctuated by coarse ridges suggesting the beginnings of a fracture, a place of weakness. Prepubescent cats for a week I can just about cope with. I pull, absorbed in the friction between my fingers, skimming the bumps, soothed by the monotony. Dylan, actively gay and my oldest friend, suddenly (*Yes! All right, Matt, not over-night, but you know what I mean*) acquiring a lifetime commitment to children he'll raise as his own is altogether different. I take the shaft of hair in my left hand, inching my way along it with my right, scoring it with my thumbnail, enjoying the resistance between hair cuticle and finger, making the hair curl like scissors scrolling ribbon for a parcel. If I increase the pressure just slightly, I'll hear the hair snap at its point of tension, split ends feathering into existence.

Instead, tonight I pull the strand right out of my scalp. I feel the root tear from its follicle, feel the small bead of pain, see the bulb's creamy globule of oil wobble in the air as I exhale. The planes of my face in the mirror are harsh yet strangely passive, my untugged hair flat and closely cropped (I am going through a vague Mia Farrow phase). I am aware of a fierce ache in my upper arms.

Chapter Four

'I DON'T KNOW WHY you're worrying, yaar,' sighs Nicole, easing a column of chocolate hair over her shoulder. 'Dylan's gay. He'll never be approved.'

I stop tipping my chair, and watch my colleague drink her first iced coffee of Monday morning. Such breaks are rare. We work hard, as headhunters, recruiting to fill senior corporate vacancies. It's not exactly rocket science, but I've got the knack of helping people fit together. Pity I had no joy with my parents.

I've decided this morning to confide in Nicole – hence the caffeine break. Nicole and I are the only female partners in the firm. We wear linen trouser suits and hide our laptops in grosgrain handbags, which sit at our feet like spaniels.

'What do you mean, *approved* ?'

'Well, adoption agencies are very picky.' Nicole's voice, as much as her sentiment, soothes me. Her New Delhi lilt always sounds intelligent and precise; it makes me believe her implicitly. 'They prefer you to be under thirty. Which Dylan, like us, is not. And married, which Dylan could claim to be, but only to a higher being.' Nicole sips her drink through beautiful, cushioned lips. 'And you must be deemed sensible, na, which Dylan most definitely hasn't been since he tried to become treasurer of the College Boat Club—'

'Only because he fancied the cox. Dylan couldn't move through water if you sewed on an outboard motor. But he's a *vicar*.'

'Absolutely. And you have to be straight.'

'Seriously?'

Nicole sets her drink down on my desk blotter and proceeds to finger-comb her hair. 'Actually, I'm not sure about that one. He could go abroad, where the rules aren't so strict.'

I choke on a mouthful of coffee. 'You mean, he might get a child from overseas?'

'Absolutely!' laughs Nicole, picking up her cup again and noisily sucking a mixture of chilled milk and air through the straw. 'But stop being so xenophobic, yaar? We foreigners aren't quite as awful as you might think. And Dylan's bound to make you godmother. How many would that make in your portfolio?'

'Six, at last count.'

Nicole pouts her approval. 'How on earth do you tell them apart?'

'It's all on a spreadsheet.'

'Achha? A spreadsheet.' We both laugh – Nicole because she assumes I'm joking, and me because I know I'm not.

'Of course, it doesn't just feature godchildren. It records all the kids of people I know. Look.' I click my mouse and, when I've located the right file, swivel the screen to Nicole. I list out the columns: 'Date of birth, full name (including Hebrew alternatives where appropriate), eye colour, presents bought, presents requested, hobbies, allergies—'

'Ye-gods!' says Nicole, in that slangy, old-fashioned Hinglish of hers that I adore. 'Boys' names in blue, girls' in red?'

'And duplicates are underlined.'

'Don't you get bored of being so anal?'

My skin prickles. I have to remind myself that Nicole is my friend. 'Don't all godmothers do this?'

'Dominic was made a godfather once, but he can't remember who to.'

'Oh, right. You and Dominic still—?'

'On and off, yaar. Can't remember why, but there we are. Probably something to do with the fact that he doesn't keep banging on about having kids.'

I smile. With that defiant, if suspiciously un-English, 'e' (Nicole's parents spent their honeymoon in the former French colony of Pondicherry), Nicole was apparently often overheard as a child voicing a desire to grow up to be an expensive toy. A First in Psychology and a successful career appear not to have dimmed such ambition.

*

During the morning, my mood seesaws. Interviewing candidates, or phoning them to tell them they've got the job, are absorbing tasks. Also, my dad rings, to let me know that he and Audrey got home safely this morning. We chat, although I steer clear of mentioning Dylan's announcement. But, between one task and the next, panic flares up like toothache in a cavity. Dylan is planning to have children. How could he! And, how could he – in the sense of how will it happen? I grip the sides of my desk until my knuckles are tinged with white.

My friends fall into two camps: not gay and straight, as Matt once scientifically observed, but child-ful and child-free. On the one side, I'm aware of an ever-increasing regiment of wailing, overtired creatures, whose self-obsessed behaviour is acted out in the name of their demanding offspring. On the other side stand Matt and me.

Our outriders are Dylan and Nicole, flanked by Jenny and Clive, who, despite being the first of my college gang to marry, have never seemed inclined to spawn. Which we all tease them about, since one would fear for children born to a father with

25

such a droopy, unfashionable moustache and a mother who has a penchant for bright, voluminous knitwear. Clive is a skinny management consultant. There is something of the angle-poise about him. Jenny is not skinny. She has an amazing singing voice, mellifluous with a rasp to it, honey dripping over the honeycomb. But she is one of life's mice; and I have always been privately intrigued, given her size, how easily someone as talented as Jenny can recede into the background. Perhaps that's why she favours such raucous jumpers.

That Dylan is now switching sides constitutes, in my humble opinion, an act of extraordinary selfishness and betrayal.

*

'So, yaar, what have you bought the twins?' asks Nicole, extracting a pack of moist tissues from her bag and wiping her manicured fingers before tackling her sandwich. (*We regret to inform you of the temporary closure today of the staff canteen due to staff training.*)

'They asked for guitars,' I reply, as I prise open a tub of salad and select the one cherry tomato. We have both had our respective client lunches cancelled and are relishing the freedom of eating without cutlery. 'Serena and Harry will kill me.'

Nicole shakes her head. 'Serena won't. With five daughters in the house, another hundred decibels won't make that much difference. And Harry won't notice – he's a teacher. He's congenitally oblivious to group disruption. Nicole dabs at the corners of her mouth. 'Now, ask me what I've bought them. I have bought', she continues excitedly, 'a bead kit for Eloise to braid her hair, and glittery playing cards for Esme. And, unlike you,

I'm not even their godmother. I am so kind!' she laughs. 'Those children will remember my presents for the rest of their lives.'

'Don't be daft. Do you remember what your godparents gave you when you were five?'

'Not much need for godparents, given that several generations of my dad's family all lived together in the same compound in Delhi.'

I struggle to imagine what having lots of relations around must feel like. Both my sets of grandparents died in the war, neither my dad nor my mother has siblings, and by the time I was four my parents had lost touch with the couple they'd made my godparents.

'But that's not the point,' continues Nicole. 'These girls will remember me—'

'—when they're in therapy with Matt,' I laugh, 'whingeing about the stereotypical presents they got as kids. We scar them for life! We buy them the presents we wish we'd had as children. And, when they grow up, they'll do exactly the same.'

'At least we *give* presents and bother to show up for parties, na. Remember last year? Very bad form to forget a godchild's birthday. Still, Ed was single back then. I wonder if he'll make it to the party this afternoon in person, or simply delegate to the lovely Louisa.'

I stop chewing. 'Ed won't be at the party.' I fork my salad leaves lazily, whilst Nicole prods my arm, demanding clarification. 'You and I are collecting Louisa *en route*.'

'So he's coming on later?'

'Ed's left Louisa.'

'Achha! When? How?'

'Last week. On a plane. With his new woman.'

'Ye-gods! Typical Ed. He's so fickle.'

'And Louisa's so pregnant.'

Nicole's beautiful brown eyes widen. 'So that's why we haven't seen them for months!'

We pick at our meal in silence, although my appetite, at least, has dwindled. It seems the only thing to do.

Chapter Five

THE NIGHT I wore my white jeans and cooked him *coq au vin*, Matt told me about his sister. When he was six years old, nearly seven, his parents told him they were going to have a lovely surprise, a miracle – which turned out not to be the genuine Springboks rugby shirt he'd been begging for, but instead a brother or sister, and Matt could choose the name. He called the baby-to-be Lesothosaurus, after his toy dinosaur, but his parents said it had to be a proper name, and began calling the bump Carl or Hannah, depending on whether it was kicking in Mummy's tummy or just fluttering. But Matt did get to help paint the room overlooking the orange orchards as a nursery, and got to tell all his friends at school that a baby was coming in time for Christmas.

And one night the baby came, although Harvest Festival was only just over. Matt woke to the sounds of a wounded animal groaning, and people running up and down the corridor. When he opened his door, the maid Phoebe rumbled past him in a blur of blue cotton, carrying the huge saucepan she used for making stews, and slopping water on to her large maroon slippers and the carpet. The howling got louder, followed by low moans, and seemed to be coming from his parents' bedroom. Lesothosaurus in his hand, Matt was about to check out the source of the noise, when his father burst out of the room, pushing Phoebe in front of him, and screaming at her to get more water, more towels. Phoebe heaved her frame down the corridor and, when she passed Matt standing in his doorway, the tears streaming down made her black face all shiny.

'Don't shout at Phoebe,' he yelled at his father, and slammed shut his bedroom door. He went to sleep with his hands over his ears.

In the morning, his father came and sat on his bed. His hair was all messed up and his eyes were bloodshot, the same as when he and the farm manager would return from a day in Johannesburg, selling oranges at auction. His father said he was sorry for shouting and he hoped that Matt would forgive him. And then he screwed a clump of blanket in his fist, and told Matt about his little sister, a delicate angel too good for this world, who had come for a visit and then gone away.

His father was looking at the wall. Matt had an uncomfortable churning feeling in his tummy. So, with his hand clutching Lesothosaurus under the bedclothes, he asked in a whisper whether he was going to be sent away soon, too. And his father had fled the room.

Chapter Six

*D*EARLY BELOVED.

Dylan married Matt and me in his church. The building squats in a cul-de-sac like a toad, between a 1960s tower block and a derelict candle factory. Carbon black from decades of grime, its buttresses and stumpy spire are as warts on a natterjack. But appearances can be deceptive. Inside, there's a reredos of beaten gold beneath a dado of carved alabaster. From the nave, one's eye is drawn high above the altar to a triptych of stained-glass windows, representing in glowing colours the Father, Son and Holy Ghost of the Trinity. In their design are patterns of such richness and dreamlike unreality that each window blends into one harmonious composition. They are windows of such beauty they feature in guidebooks.

Dylan enjoys the mismatch between inside and out. It symbolises for him the essence of religion, how the inner is more important than any outer show. I've never really taken much notice of the architecture. I'm drawn instead to all the drama – what Dylan calls the smells and bells. I don't have faith, as such. Haven't had since my early childhood prayers went unanswered.

My faith is in Dylan.

Do you, Amber?

We met at university, reading English. Dylan, with his explosion of ginger curls, favoured contemporary writers, and embraced deconstruction. Back then I wore my hair in a ponytail, and found comfort in the formal social codes of Dickens and James. Dylan read voraciously, scribbling frantic notes and disagreements in the margins, cracking the spines as he splayed the books, the better to devour and digest the words. I bought little plastic covers for my books, and kept their spines in mint condition.

Mesmerised in lectures by Dylan's habit of scrawling the letters 'AMDG' at the top of all his notes, I was in awe of his devotion to God. I imagined a life rich with spiritual meaning. Later I learned this was a misconception, that it was in fact a ritual left over from a failed love affair with a Catholic boy in the village.

Do you take this man?

If I now attend church at all, it's to enjoy the changing altar drapes of the church year; to be moved by the sight of Dylan's hands placed on the heads of children, their hair enamelled by the wands of light filtering through the stained glass; or to see his arms raised for the final blessing, striking the pose he once adopted as Salieri in a college production of *Amadeus*. I go out of friendship, although I suspect that something in the church's quiet rhythm, its annual calendar or its daily rituals, has drawn me in. A toad catching a fly.

For our wedding, Jenny, in a yellow cashmere cardigan chosen to match the freesias in my bouquet, sang Sondheim's 'Being Alive', a performance so moving that the congregation felt compelled to clap. And Dylan delivered a sermon, urging us to take the risk, and find the joy in each other.

Do you promise?

*

'So, we never finished talking about Ed and Louisa, na,' says Nicole, switching off the intercom to stop the taxi driver listening. 'What else did she tell you?'

'Said he phoned from the airport, to say that he needed to sort a few things out, and that she ought to think about an abortion.'

'Eeshhh!' says Nicole, reaching into her grosgrain handbag for a comb. 'He cuts to the chase. And Louisa said?'

'Nothing much. Hang on – excuse me, it's right at the next lights, and then second on the left. Where was I? Oh yes, and her mother's staying with her in Ed's flat.'

'But is Louisa going to keep the baby? That's the most pressing thing, surely?'

'I got the feeling it's all a bit late for that.'

'Catholic?' asks Nicole, combing at a particularly resilient knot.

'No, just too late all round. Poor girl.'

'No wonder we haven't seen them for months.' We both stare thoughtfully out of our respective windows of the taxi. 'So, approaching forty obviously hasn't made Ed grow up.'

'Yeah, midlife crisis,' I say. 'And his secretary's also taken the week off. Yes, where that mini's parked, thank you. Look, Louisa's on the doorstep. She must have heard us turning into the street. Oh the poor thing – she looks exhausted,' I add.

Nicole opens the taxi door and steps on to the pavement. 'Hello Lou. Look, leave that bag on the pavement, I'll get it. You step in.'

I register the stony pallor of Louisa's skin. It emphasises her wide, green eyes. 'Hi, Lou. Do you want to sit facing the driver?"

'Thank you, Amber, yes,' she says, heaving herself in with effort. Her high voice, with its refined elocution, sounds watered down somehow. 'I still get queasy, even this late in the afternoon.' Her lips barely part as she speaks, as if she's scared she might throw up at any moment. I want to hold her, rub her back or something, but I'm afraid I'll make her feel worse.

As our taxi pulls away, I catch a glimpse of a woman at the

ground-floor window, who I take to be Louisa's mother. I watch her as she runs her finger along the sash. Turning her palm upwards, she inspects the dust on the tip, before pressing it on to the windowpane, a fingerprint at the scene of the crime – the scene of Ed's treachery. *If you mess with my daughter*, this gesture seems to say, *you mess with me.*

Till death us do part.

*

And then we were husband and wife. There was champagne for the reception, and sea bass for supper. Everyone had a lump in their throat when Dad recalled when I was small enough to lie on his forearm, between fingertip and the crook of his elbow. And my mother, sitting at a separate table, had apparently remarked to no one in particular that actually her ex-husband was wrong, and that I was a very long baby – rather like the labour.

And Matt's best man, fellow medic Peder, had told lots of stories as fed to him by old chums like Dylan; stories which resolved important urban mysteries such as why he was known at boarding school as 'Fat Matt' despite being very slim and fit (answer: because no one could ever pronounce his real name, a custom his friends had praised me for overturning). And people had written rude things in our guest book, and taken mad photos of each other with disposable cameras. And I was introduced by my new mother-in-law, who was wearing nuptial black, to a distant uncle over from South Africa – and the uncle kept referring to my new husband as Matthys, but my new mother-in-law had explained that we all had to call him Matt from now on because poor Amber can't pronounce Matthys.

For better, for worse.

*

Harry opens the door and several small children push past his legs. They thud into the three of us standing on the path. Harry blinks to attention.

'Girls, girls, girls. What a treat!' he enthuses, his voice carrying its habitual note of irony, as if he isn't surrounded on a daily basis by females.

I scoop up Eloise, one of Harry's five daughters, and balance her on my hip. Her floppy blonde hair smells of strawberries, and for a moment I turn my head slightly to inhale this scent in secret. My heart melts. She giggles and tells me I'm tickling her ear. She pulls at my face to make it face hers again. The skin at her temples is pale and delicate, nearly transparent. I marvel at the way she literally seizes what she wants from life. I want her never to lose this. I squeeze her tightly.

Eloise leans forward to pat Louisa's distended stomach.

'Pat gently, Ellie,' I say. 'Louisa has a baby in her tummy.'

'For me?' Eloise asks. 'I'm six,' she adds, as if this statement provides ample justification for Louisa handing over her one remaining reason for living.

'Well, birthday girl,' I say quickly, 'let's go in and see all the presents you've had.'

*

Our present table resembled something out of central casting. A dry-stone wall of boxes wrapped in shiny paper, shapes almost too perfect to contain real gifts. Frankly, I was flattered; I'd had dreams in the run-up to the wedding of walking down the aisle surrounded by empty pews.

We decided against a wedding list: the prerogative of marrying in our thirties. I suggested this because I feared our guests would overlook it. Matt agreed, and told me he hoped to offer the absence of a wedding list as a symbol to his parents of his autonomy. Above all, such was our faith in our relationship that to ask for something as mundane as a set of kitchen steps verged on the sacrilegious.

And yet, given the pile of presents we received, I could only conclude that guests had been wracked with guilt at the prospect of arriving empty-handed, or had felt under some compulsion to demonstrate by their well-judged gifts just what good friends they were of ours, of Matt and me, the new Bezeidenhouts. During the reception, Dylan had sent four choir boys to the church hall to collect trestle tables and erect them at the back of the marquee pitched in the vicar-cage garden.

By the power vested in me.

*

Dylan and Jenny loiter with poorly disguised intent beside the sausages on sticks; hardly surprising, since Dylan can't cook, and Jenny can never stop eating (she says she's too attached to the Mondrian patterns on her poncho jumpers to diet). Eloise is still joined to my hip, while Esme hits my bottom with a cushion. Serena approaches with a plate daubed with crumbs and smudges of buttercream.

'You two! I wondered who was squirrelling all the sausages away. I don't know! The children only want to eat sweet things this year.'

'It was Jenny,' mumbles Dylan, chewing. Jenny slaps Dylan playfully and, during the ensuing laughter, pops another sausage into her mouth.

'I can never keep up,' laughs Serena. 'At Eleanor's party it was Hula Hoops, and at Emily's it was egg sarnies. There's always one item of food the children want to eat above all else. And this year it's cake. At this rate, we're going to be eating sausages until next Christmas.'

'Not if Dylan keeps this up,' I laugh, setting Eloise down.

'Dylan, dearest, can you be an angel and herd everyone into the sitting room. Harry's about to do his clown thing and the kids never listen to me.'

'Only', says Dylan, handing her his glass of boxed wine, 'if you guard this till I get back.'

Serena agrees, while Dylan walks over in the manner of a ghoul to a group of children.

'Shouldn't really,' whispers Serena, placing a palm over the glass. Jenny and I stare at her.

'You're not?' we both chime.

'No, no, no,' Serena giggles. 'I can't be. I'm on the pill. Harry made me, after number five. No, it's just that I'm so tired. Still, what the heck!' She takes a long mouthful and places the glass on the table. 'Although, don't say anything, but I stopped last month.'

'You stopped taking the pill?' asks Jenny, as if to clarify. Her honey-fed tones sound coarser somehow.

'Shhhhhh. Yes. But don't tell Harry.'

'You old devil!' I say, regarding my friend. Not for the first time, I wonder what it must be like to be Serena, to have let yourself go physically, producing so many children in quick succession, and to not mind. To have permanently chapped hands, and thick ankles, and bags under the eyes, and to not have time to visit the hairdressers to mask the grey. To be barely able to tie an apron around your shapeless middle – to be too busy, perhaps, to ever take the apron *off*. Now, there's an intriguing contraceptive. Instinctively I tighten my stomach muscles. I have memorised, without realising, the duration of Serena's four labours (the most recent baby was practically born in the hospital lift). The drama of the twins' emergency Caesarean, for example, is seared into my mind. The most remarkable thing is that Serena never complains, not about the piles, not about the nausea, not about her girls. To spend every day juggling crisis and heartache and anarchy, and to do it all for love? That, I believe, is the most mysterious part of all.

'But you've got five already,' says Jenny, taking a step back.

'I know, I know. And Harry's been talking lately about vasectomies. Someone in his staffroom has had one and says it's done wonders for his sex life—'

'Evidence would suggest', I say, 'that you and Harry need hardly worry on that score—'

''Fraid not, Amber. I'm just gloriously fertile! But I was in the attic sorting out things for this party and I came across a bag of baby clothes. I took them out and began to fold them properly with a view to giving them to charity, and I realised that I couldn't do it. All those pink clothes, the tiny dresses. How could I give them away? It would be like giving away my own children. I sat in that attic for an hour and sobbed.'

'Poor you,' I say, putting a tentative arm around her. The warmth, the softness of Serena's body surprises me – while her back feels strong, as do her shoulder blades. It's as if she is more real, more genuine than me.

'Oh, Amber, you're sweet. But I know I'm lucky. Some women can't conceive. They're desperate. Imagine that. Every day I look at the girls and I can't help smiling. But you career women don't want to hear me blather on about my addiction to soiled nappies. See! Where's Jenny gone? I've been boring you all and she's escaped! Come on. Let's go and see if Harry's Clarence the Clown is keeping them quiet.'

As Serena follows me into the other room, she creeps up and whispers in my ear, 'But I tell you, if Harry *is* planning a vasectomy, he'd better be bloody quick!'

*

I enter the kitchen having read the twins one final bedtime story, smiling at the memory of Eloise and Esme asleep in separate beds, holding hands across the carpet. Serena is spooning coffee granules into mugs. Dylan is stretching cling film over margarine tubs overflowing with cheese straws and crisps, a talent honed by fifteen years of parish soirées. Harry stands at the sink wiping clown make-up from his face with own-brand kitchen towels.

I accept a mug from Serena, decline milk, and breathe in the muskiness. After the brittle noises of the party, I relax in the silence between friends. Everyone else has gone home: Nicole braved a cab with queasy Louisa, and Jenny left early to cook supper, or knit a sweater.

I watch Harry as I sip, remembering another performance, another lifetime, before babies, before clients, before choices. Harry as Prospero, Harry as King Lear, Harry as Joe Keller. Harry reading Sky to my Sarah in *Guys and Dolls* – a production that was cancelled early due to lack of funds. It's as if Harry was always destined to play only the father.

I met Dylan and Harry at auditions for the university revue

group. My thoughts turn to plays performed, curtains called, and I compare them instantaneously, as the mind can, to the competitiveness of work. And I wonder how I was seduced into trading in the simple pleasure of applause for the flashier model of a competitive package with performance-related bonus. As I watch Harry throw the last traces of his clown's face into the bin, I marvel at his faith in being able to delight his children.

'Sweet one, you were tremendous,' says Serena, handing her husband his coffee.

'Praise indeed from the Butcher of Battersea!' he smiles, and they clink chipped mugs. Behind them, the lights on the baby monitor flare like a rash, a child's whimper getting louder.

'Yes,' says Dylan, 'I was going to say, Hal. Your finest performance ever!'

'Well, Dyl, you've got to do your bit,' says Serena, heading for the door. 'Children's parties are so competitive now, and we can't afford a professional entertainer. For richer, for poorer, eh?' Here she winks at Harry. 'So, you do what you have to do. I'll go, Harry. You stay and drink your coffee.'

I hear her steady footsteps as she climbs the stairs.

'Seeing as how you obviously haven't lost your old touch, Hal, I've got the parish drama group staging *Company* at Harvest Festival this year. I've tried to persuade Amber to audition. Maybe you'd like to? You could say I'm hoping to harvest the fruit of your talents!'

'*Company*?' says Harry, thoughtfully. 'Isn't that the Sondheim show about the chap who's surrounded by married friends, but who's afraid to get hitched?'

'The very same,' says Dylan. 'A man under pressure! Fancy it?'

'I'm sorry, Dyl. I'm under enough pressure this summer. I swear,

I do much more work than any of my pupils, and I'm sure that's not the right way round—'

'Oh, go on—'

'He's got five children, Dylan,' I add.

'And, of course we'd have more, if I had my way—'

'More?' Dylan and I say, cautiously, together.

'So, if I'm going to—'

'Did you mean more money, or more work?' I say, a little too sharply, knowing he didn't mean either, but resisting the appalling alternative.

'No,' says Harry, quietly. 'More children.' And he reaches up into a top cupboard and brings down an old bottle of whisky.

'You sly old dog,' cries Dylan. 'Last week you told me, in confidence, that you were thinking of having the snip.'

'I know. I was. The head of Biology has had one and—'

'Intentionally? Or a class experiment which went badly wrong?'

'Shut up, Dyl,' I snap. 'Does Serena know how you feel?' I pour a finger, and drink it back in one gulp.

'Well, she's on the pill, so it's not really an issue.' Harry stares down at his shoes and shuffles his feet away from an imaginary finishing line on the lino. 'But, you know, I was looking at the faces of all the children this afternoon, their eyes shining like conkers, and it brought it all back to me. I so loved being a child, didn't you? Every day was so exciting, full of adventure. I think I want to put off the day that stops happening in this house.'

I grab the bottle and pour myself another slug.

'At this rate, by the time you stop, your oldest will be producing grandchildren!' laughs Dylan, putting his arm around Harry.

'Well, that's what it's all about, isn't it?' I can see his eyes are shining. 'I have such clear memories. Like having chickenpox one June, and my father teaching me to bowl in the fortnight I was off school. Bowling at a wicket painted on the back wall, over, and over, and over again. Off-spinners, leg breaks. God, that was the best summer ever. And Ian Botham being sacked as captain against Australia, and then making two centuries, and taking five wickets to win the series. And seeing *Twenty Thousand Leagues Under the Sea*. And visiting HMS *Victory* in dry dock in Portsmouth and discovering that the floorboards of the lowest deck where the surgeon worked were painted red to hide the blood. Those were wonderful days, wonderful days. I don't want to lose that. I loved it so much, I want it all over again.' He looks from Dylan to me and grins shyly, as if seeking affirmation. 'I want a son.'

*

I close my front door and rest against it. I can still smell Dylan's cologne where we cheek-hugged goodnight. He declined my offer of coffee; he has a sermon to write, and a suitcase to pack for tomorrow's retreat. My stomach, even after tonight's diet of party food, rumbles vigorously. The house is in darkness. Tallulah (*or is it timid Tim? Who gives a toss?*) tiptoes into the hall and swirls herself, himself, around my legs. The fur against my tights sets my teeth on edge. My mother says cats gravitate to those who like them least. How fortunate, I think, that in human relationships it's the other way around.

I've never been nervous before about discussing things with Dylan. There's never been any censorship. We've survived meeting each other's mothers, for goodness sake; what more evidence of friendship do you need? And yet, tonight, I was conscious of the word hanging in the car between us, as annoying as furry dice.

Adoption. Yet I know I must say something soon. I want specifics. Above all, I think I want him to tell me it was all a joke.

In the kitchen, the answer machine is winking at me. It'll be Matt's caramel voice explaining, in vague terms, the crisis currently rendering me a work widow. I feel an irrational stab of envy for the patients commanding his attention. I want the man they call a saint to be my saviour alone.

Before I have a chance to play his message, the doorbell rings. I pad up to the hall. Matt must have left his keys at the hospital.

'The cats!' wails Dylan, pushing past me. His melodrama isn't even feigned.

'What about them?' I ask, through tight lips.

'Well, I could hardly go on retreat without saying goodbye!'

'They've been suicidal,' I say, drily. Dylan laughs at what he imagines is sarcasm. Suddenly, I can't bear for Dylan to find them. 'They just left.'

I watch a frown crumple Dylan's forehead as he thinks this through. This is my power, the power to make Dylan pause and reflect. But he'd never understand, would never choose me over the cats, would never even realise he was expected to make a choice. And all because I can never tell anyone of my fear that there never seems to be enough love to go round.

As he calls their names, Tallulah enters the hall. She sidles up to his legs and curls herself around them. She half-lowers her eyelids, and lets out a seductive purr of encouragement. Dylan picks her up. I scrunch my toes on the sisal.

'So, you hadn't come to see me, then?' I say, going downstairs to the kitchen. I'm aiming for levity, but recognise it, once vocalised, as a handbrake turn on the slip road to hysteria. I busy myself making drinks and stand close to the kettle. In the background, Dylan is making baby talk. He is so engrossed in his reunion that it's not until I slam his mug down on a pile of rejected CVs that he starts to communicate with me and admits that he really can't stay.

'Just for a few minutes.' My whine revolts me. But at just this moment, Tallulah (*she's probably killed Tim*) leaps from Dylan's arms. So he agrees to stay, and sips his coffee.

'God,' he groans, wiping the back of his hand across his eyes, which are watering profusely. 'Imagine having to entertain kids all day, every day. I don't know how Serena and Harry do it.'

I eye him carefully. 'I reckon they find it hard, finding time for each other.' I want to speak on, but something makes me hesitate, knowing Dylan will never fully understand my bizarre fears of being replaced in his affections by two *cats*. Dylan, son of Pamela, who married young and produced her little prince before she was out of her teens. As Matt once put it to me: unable to tolerate the competition, Dylan's father had died of a heart attack when our Oedipus was less than two. Dylan has Pamela.

I've never known such certainty.

'Do you know your answer machine's flashing?' says Dylan, suddenly. He leans over and hits the play button. Which on reflection is a good thing, as it means that I'm not alone as I listen to Audrey's voice, letting me know, with much sorrow, that my father has died.

Chapter Seven

ILIE AWAKE. My neck feels stiff. My pillow is wet. The street outside is silent – we're having to sleep with the windows open because of the heat – as is the flight path. An opal light steals through a gap in the curtains. Fresh tears dribble out of my eyes and slide into my ears.

I am remembering how, when I first showed Dad my engagement ring, he'd brought it to his lips and kissed it. He will never see it again, will never phone here again and wheeze a message into our answer machine. I will never again feel his embrace.

He died from an aneurysm, but they couldn't operate. Audrey, when I phoned her last night, explained that the drug in Dad's system, skittling around his blood to prevent further strokes, was the same anti-clotting agent that made surviving surgery impossible. He has, I feel, been cheated by science. An act of bad faith that confirms my worst fears: that diligent planning counts for nothing. After I put the phone down, I had a vision of Audrey doing the same thing in her flat. Beside her phone stands one of his vases; I bet she stroked it once we'd finished our call.

I used to love watching him throw pots on the wheel. His studio was at the back of our semi, where Mother would have preferred a sunroom. Its walls were covered with postcard reproductions, and yellowing articles torn from newspapers; reviews of exhibitions to be visited; interviews with artists. Many were marked with stars, in his red biro.

I never stopped being amazed by how he could make things so solid, so permanent, from lumps of clay – pots, vases, even a tea service. The whole process fascinated me: rolling up his sleeves, selecting clay from the plastic-lidded dustbin he kept outside; weighing lumps in his hand, feeling their density, their elasticity; removing all the air bubbles to stop the pot exploding in the kiln, which he did by slamming it down on his table, and which I was allowed to do when I got bigger, cutting it in half with cheese wire to check for further air bubbles, and kneading it like bread.

Perched on the corner of Dad's table, or rather on piles of colour supplements, I'd watch him preparing the wheel – wetting the plate, kicking the pedal, getting it to the right speed. Once he was sitting comfortably with his thighs either side, he would slam the clay on to the plate, right in the middle, never missing. Then he'd kick the pedal, cradle the clay, and slop water gently over it, monitoring it closely, keeping his body firm (letting the clay know who's boss, he called it); and from nowhere a smooth ball would emerge, and then a glistening cone, a stalagmite. And then, using his left hand to keep things steady, he used his right middle finger and thumb to create a well in the clay, pulling it up, slowly, carefully, until he had the shape he wanted.

I have a couple of those vases still.

I turn over. Beside me, Matt emits the settled breaths of deep sleep. I feel an ache in my chest. I long to cradle his head, and stroke the short, sandy hairs on his earlobes, or the butterscotch skin of his shoulders – like an object of holy reverence whose halo shines too brightly. I hesitate to reach out. I loved my dad and he is gone.

Finally, Matt opens his eyes. I like to think his sixth sense knew I was watching. He grins at me, and reaches out to wipe away some tears with a finger. 'So sad,' he whispers.

I sort of nod into the pillow.

'How long have you been crying?' he whispers.

It's a simple question, with a solid answer. It makes Matt seem very wise, very safe; a sage who has been around for centuries. It's how I know I can tell Matt anything, and he will not be destroyed, by my guilt, by my pain. I want to speak, but I keep remembering my father's last chat with me, telling me he'd phone this weekend. I want to punch the headboard. Instead, I can feel more tears leaking out. Matt pulls me to him, and strokes my hair over and over again.

*

After Matt's sister died, Matt's mother struggled to leave her bedroom. When she did, it was to snap at Phoebe, or to take long baths. And yet to Matt it was as though she had for ever locked away a part of herself in the wardrobe – the part that used to laugh, and smile, and make orange curd, and sunbathe at the pool. Sometimes she got dressed, sometimes she didn't; she shouted at her husband, and harangued the garden boys: the proteas had leaf blight, the bobotie was too dry, the sun was too hot, too cold.

At first, Matt was the only one she never shouted at. When he came home in the afternoon from school, she would look into his eyes and ask about his achievements, before rushing off to lie down. Over time, he found it necessary to up his game, to be not just a member of the cricket team but to be its captain, if he was to feel her touch at all; and avoid the lingering fear that he might be dismissed, like his sister.

Matt was sent to school in England when he was eleven; his paternal grandparents had now emigrated there, and they were paying. By then his mother was taking a variety of pills, which she complained made her mouth dry, or gave her insomnia. Every year, around Harvest Festival, she would announce that she was done with them for good, and make a show of throwing them away. Within two or three days she could be found on her hands and knees, sobbing uncontrollably, and a doctor had to drive twenty kilometres out to the farm to sedate her, and tweak her medication. And Matt would return home for the holidays to find a woman he barely recognised.

When he was fifteen, Matt won the science prize – a book of Freud's collected works. In his study, beneath a poster for *Led Zeppelin IV*, he'd lie on his bed, devouring the essays, digesting their often bitter relevance. Here was someone making sense of his world, answering questions he wasn't aware he'd longed to ask. Hungrily, he turned to others: to Laing, Klein, Winnicott, who shone their torches into the crevices of the human mind and soul. In reading these writers and their case studies, Matt felt somehow closer to himself, the mother he lost, and to the sister he never knew.

Matt was a junior house officer when, on a visit back to the farm, he saw the number of pills his mother took at each meal, and made discreet enquiries about therapy groups in the area. The nearest was thirty kilometres away in Nelspruit. Matt met the facilitator, and sat in on a group. He told his parents it was a book club; something neither of them had attended, and therefore a fact neither of them could dispute.

And once a week his mother drives to Nelspruit, and sits in a circle, and talks and listens, without realising she's taking part in therapy at all.

*

After we make love, Matt dozes, I get up, slip on a T-shirt and head downstairs. In the kitchen, I light a rare cigarette from an old packet of Dylan's and, taking a ramekin for the ash, sit on the step of the French windows, channelling smoke into the garden. The flag-stones beneath my feet are already warm; it's going to be another hot one.

I hardly ever smoke and, when I do, it's only after sex. I giggle at the cliché – I don't even own a lighter. Since talk of either activity earned my mother's reproach, it seemed only fitting that the night I felt brave enough to cadge my first cigarette (from Angus, fellow Saturday worker at the local Marks and Spencer) was the same night I lost my virginity (good old Angus), these twin totems of so-called maturity for ever commissioned together in my memory, conspirators in a long-standing war of attrition.

I take a drag, swirl the dryness around my mouth, and slowly exhale, watching the smoke evaporate, leaving behind only a bitter taste. *I'll call you at the weekend.* I grind the stub into the ramekin.

I am reminded of an article I read recently which said that death in a family is often followed by a birth. I scrabble for another cigarette. With the muscle memory of Matt inside me, what if I'm pregnant? And for one brief moment the flutter of panic in my chest seems so unbridled, so engulfing, so hard to swallow down, that I reckon this must be what it feels like to be one of Matt's patients, my rivals for Matt's attention.

Before I've had a chance to light a new ciggie, Matt's voice reaches me from across the kitchen. 'Heyyy!' he says in that way he has of greeting me which makes this one syllable sound as though with my presence all his prayers have been answered.

'Ach, man! Smoke,' he complains, on kissing me, before sitting between my legs.

A cat (*get lost, rodent)* sprints with a rustle from the foliage to rub itself against my darling husband's shins.

'Hello, boy,' Matt enthuses, vigorously scratching its underbelly.

'How do you know it's the boy one?' I say, trying to steady my voice and sound normal and curious, not fraught and jealous.

'Tim? Because it looks like Tim.' Just occasionally, Matt's spring-bok lilt will hint at a subtext of *Yes, my wife is daft as a brush.* I bet he doesn't use that tone at work.

'But how can you tell them apart?' Briefly my curiosity outweighs my anxiety.

Matt cranes his neck to look back up at me. 'Well, wife. Could it be, as my patients tell me, that I'm a genius? Or that the cats look different? Now, let's examine the evidence. Tim has white patches on his face—' Matt turns back to the cat and buries his face in the fur. 'Yes, you do! And Tallulah is—' here Matt pauses, '—totally ginger. But, you're right. It's tricky!'

I snap the cigarette I'm holding. My husband is engrossed in tick-ling the cat. I open my mouth and close it again. It's hard to confess to the one you love that you feel threatened by cats, especially female ones; that you fear they are your rivals in love.

I have to wait a good five minutes before Matt says, 'Now bugger off, Tim. I want to hug my wife.' He moves to sit on my step and pulls me towards him. I kiss his collarbone. He smells of sleep.

'You know now Dad's gone, I'm going to have to—' My throat tightens and I can't speak.

'Get in touch with your mother? Yah, but not until after the funeral,' whispers Matt, repeating what Audrey told us of Dad's liv-ing will. 'Be grateful for some breathing space.'

The will instructs me to delay informing mother of his death. Matt reckons Dad wanted to stop her turning up at the crematorium.

Matt circles me in the welcome billet of his arms. The sun is higher now, its golden wash sloping casually over the top of the garden wall. I am still in the shade, but a lozenge of light brushes half of Matt's body, burnishing the tawny hairs on his skin, so that he appears as the luminous source of all that is good and safe in the world.

Chapter Eight

LATER THAT MORNING, the sky has changed. It is the weak blue and yellow of old people's eyes. From my office on the first floor of a building in Bond Street, I watch thin women window-shopping, gorging on nothing more than the reflection of their own bodies. I turn back to my desk and finish a chocolate bourbon.

Dominic arrives from a meeting. He sets his jacket across the back of his chair with a matador's flourish. I smirk as he glances over to Nicole's office to check whether she witnessed this performance; and I know Nicole is far too smart to let on. Several secretaries did see, however, and, although Dominic regards such women as plankton in the office food chain, it's clear to me that their visible interest affords his ego minor consolation.

Pleading the need to purchase a muffin (*we regret to inform you of the temporary closure today of the staff canteen due to a fire in the stir-fry console*), I hand a Dictaphone tape containing three candidate letters to my secretary Maxine, and wander out towards Piccadilly.

Somehow I find myself in the courtyard of the Royal Academy. An old man wearing a raincoat the colour of pigeons is shuffling slowly towards the gallery steps, has already stopped twice to catch his breath. Suddenly he topples forward. All the sinews in my body tense; another man having a stroke. But then I see that actually he's bending to rescue what is probably an insect from the flagging, carrying it cupped in his hands to a nearby urn for safety.

*

'Excuse me for asking, but is it free next to you?'

I half squint into the sun. I want to be alone. The shape looming before me, the source of this question, is male. His black shoes are shiny, with square buckles. The trousers are pinstriped – I shift my gaze away from the man's pubic bone to his suntanned hands. In one he carries a beaker of coffee; a golden disc glints at the cuff, and is scrolled with initials. I take in all this information, make my snap judgement and try to write the man off, to get back to brooding about my dad and to having a good old wallow in self-pity.

Yet I pause. The shirt sleeve at the other wrist flaps. A link is missing; the cuffs are actually frayed, as though they've been turned once too often. His skin is the colour Matt's goes when we're on holiday. And his accent is just a little too clipped. I'm shoving this man into a box, but the lid refuses to close.

'—only, there are so many kids here, it's hard to know where to perch the old B-T-M—'

The phrase makes me smile. I imagine the man learning English by watching the same old Ealing comedies I did as a child. It makes him seem very conscientious.

'—But, you know, Miss, if you're waiting for someone, I quite understand—'

'No, no. Please, feel free.' In my list of neuroses, as Matt is often telling me, my fear of disapproval has adapted to be one of the fittest. I shuffle along the wall.

'Any of these kiddies yours?' he laughs, gesturing vaguely at the crowds in the courtyard.

'No,' I reply. 'I've never wanted children.'

I blush, but the man appears not to have noticed my candour. Instead, he strides off into the conversation to ask me what I do. Normally, I prefer to be the one asking the questions. Yet, I tell him.

'I thought headhunters died out with the pygmies!'

I grin, having never heard that comment before. Or perhaps only *every* time I announce my job. Still, it's preferable to the charade of people pretending to search in their pockets for their CV. 'I only wear a bone through my nose in the privacy of my office.'

'Wish I'd brought my résumé!' he continues, patting the sides of his trousers. I have to stop myself rolling my eyes. Only the uninitiated say 'resumé'. 'I'm Fergus,' he concludes, offering a hand in the gesture of a karate player about to split bricks.

'Fergus,' I repeat, a little more interested. 'Well, that's not what I was expecting.'

'No one ever is! My mother read *Waverley* at school in Düsseldorf. She's so proud I work in London. I'm an investment banker—'

From nowhere comes an urge to shout at this man, that maybe his mother's trying to turn him into something he's not, and that he should wise up and work out who he really is. And then I realise how utterly stunned I'd be if anyone spoke to me like that, how deflated I'd feel. A wave of guilt floods my body.

And even as my head starts to throb, I'm aware of Fergus's hands gripping his beaker too tightly (*only, sadly, change is on the anvil*), of the way they relax (*since I've just been made redundant*), and then contract again (*or downsized, as they call it, which has queered my pitch*), in an almost obsessive movement (*half the department. Threw everyone into a tizzy*), of the way the liquid oozes to the top (*and I'm not yet forty*), before it squirts over his hands—

'Oh, my!' he cries, standing up abruptly, dropping the beaker, wringing his hands, flicking his wrists, and distributing globules of coffee over nearby surfaces, including my suit, his trousers and the woman sitting next to me.

Ever prepared, despite my mother's ban on joining the Brownies, I produce a pack of moist wipes. I offer it to my neighbour, who scowls and takes two, and then to Fergus. When he finishes mopping up the mess, he holds them out for me, sticky and stained. I point out a bin by the wall. His movements are awkward; he's a toddler learning to walk.

'So, what will you do?' I ask, when he returns.

'I'm currently chalking out my plans.'

'You could always go travelling. Take some time out.'

'Ah, yes. The famous gap year. I'm too old for that backpacking malarkey. And what about the rotten hole in my résumé?'

I explain that employers nowadays are terribly open-minded. 'You might give up investment banking altogether!'

'Give it up?' By the panic in his eyes, the idea is clearly on a par with being caught wetting the bed. 'You'll be telling me next to sleep under a pyramid construction. Or have people massage my feet. Give it up, eh? I'd say there's more chance of me falling pregnant!'

*

I enter the basement flat, breathing in its familiar scent of lavender. My shoulders relax. Candles flicker. A tiny, porcelain Kuan Yin figure, for compassionate feng shui, shimmers in the glow. On the coffee table stands a potted African violet.

'And how've you been this week?' murmurs Ginny, rubbing my back with firm circular movements, as I sit with my feet soaking in warm soapy water. She's a trim woman in her early sixties, although her blue eyes and smile make her look younger. Above a desk, where a laptop has sat idle for months, hangs a pin-board covered with images of Madonnas and infants, postcards of thanks, and photographs of babies. Ginny specialises in treating infertility.

As she eases me into the chair and wraps my feet in supple towels, I tell her about Dad, and the funeral arrangements. She sets to work on my right foot with gentle scudding gestures.

And suddenly my eyes sting. Because, after meeting Fergus, I entered the gallery, where I saw again the old man in the raincoat, standing close to a painting to scrutinise its brush strokes. Moments later I saw a guard grasp his shoulder, accusing the man of trying to touch the painting.

Ginny continues massaging with one hand and passes me a box of tissues with the other. 'You miss your father,' says Ginny, her knuckles grinding the crystal deposits at my heel. I squirm in my chair, and sob for some time.

'And now I'm about to lose Dylan,' I say, when I am able to dry my eyes. And I tell her about the adoption announcement.

She wraps my right foot in towelling, unwraps the left. 'Have you told him how you feel?'

I shake my head. 'Too scared,' I pout. 'And soon I'll have to contact my mother.'

'When were you two ladies last in touch?'

I have to think. 'Maybe eighteen months ago. She sends me postcards now and then, to let me know she hasn't died.'

'She wants to make contact.'

'Not so much that she phones! And when she does write, she rarely bothers to fill the postcard. She scribbles a couple of lines in her tiny writing, and then leaves a gaping space underneath.'

Outside, the evening light is fading. The day has used up its ration.

'So that makes two of you capable of giving the silent treatment!' Ginny's eyes twinkle. 'You're terrified of contacting your mother, and she's terrified—' Ginny stops.

The flutter of panic resurfaces. Ginny is being insufferably even-handed. I'm not courageous enough to enter that dark labyrinth of what might terrify my own mother.

'I'm sorry, I have to go now,' I tell her, and start writing out the cheque.

*

In Sainsbury's, struggling to think of something for supper, I stand staring at a display of dead fish on ice. Ginny's parting words ring in my ears: that Mother can no longer hurt me. I want to believe her. I really, really do. But such blind faith, worthy of one of Dylan's religious retreats, feels reckless and beyond my reach.

Chapter Nine

WHEN I WAS SEVEN, my mother went to the doctor's, feeling unwell. She took the bus because she has never learned to drive. After she'd been gone for nearly two hours, my father received a phone call from the surgery receptionist, who said that my mother was suspected of having measles and that she was being held in isolation until someone could collect her.

When my father and I arrived, we were directed to the far end of the corridor, and a room off to the left. It was painted white, although the bright, fluorescent lights made it seem almost blue. Along each wall ran a line of cupboards, their surfaces clear. Each cupboard had a black plastic safety lock looped around the handles.

Mother sat on a metal chair in the centre of the room. She still wore her coat, and held her handbag on her lap. Held it as though she would never, ever let it go. Her skin looked grey.

There was a moment before we crossed the threshold when I remember thinking how small she looked with all the whiteness around her; like a child at school whose parents have forgotten to collect them.

Chapter Ten

I'VE BEEN TOO BUSY to contact my mother. Firstly, we've had Dad's funeral: half an hour at a coastal crematorium, followed by scones and bridge rolls at Audrey's flat. Standing room only, what with all Audrey and Dad's bowls club friends in attendance. I gather they average two a week; for this crowd, funerals have become their social life. Dylan, I know, would approve. *Celebrate life*, he says. *Even in death*. Which frankly is hard to do when the person you want to celebrate with is dead. Audrey wanted me to do a reading, but I wasn't sure I could get through it without howling like a banshee, so Matt read, and I gripped Audrey's elbow throughout.

In the car on the way back to London, Matt reached out for my knee.

'Do you remember the first time I met your father?' I knew what he was going to say. 'How he shook my hand, and accidentally trapped the fleshy bit, here—' he wiggled his hand to show the webbing between thumb and forefinger, 'And as we stood chatting, your father held on to me—'

'—with his firm potter's grasp, no less!'

'—leaving me crippled with pain. I was practically on my knees!'

'Always makes me think of stags rutting,' I giggled.

It had, we agreed, been a good funeral.

The second reason for not contacting my mother is my job. I've been invited by one of my major clients to recruit the head of their

American advisory committee, although the board is insisting on a three-way *beauty parade* pitch for the business. It's the economic climate, I tell myself; it in no way reflects on my past performance. All the same, it frustrates me having to compete.

As an only child, I've always imagined myself under-practised in the art of social dynamics. Unfortunate, then, that my office seethes with sibling rivalry. All the directors compete for the attention of Rex, *in loco parentis*, he with hands the perfect size for cupping secretarial behinds; competing, more specifically, for the baubles of lucrative non-executive directorships which lie within Rex's experienced gift; competing, above all, to be anointed heir to the partnership, the ultimate symbol of his parental approbation. The role of bullying office oldest sister belongs to Julia, Rex's PA, the type of woman who wears slacks with elasticated waistbands.

As a result, the office is riddled with the woodworm of insecurity. It's assumed that women will work up to two years before giving in to their hormones. My secretary, Maxine who has, under these unspoken terms, extended her apprenticeship by several months, has already been treated to two of Rex's little lunches, his infamous *tête-à-têtes*, designed to plant the seed (I trust the phrase is purely metaphorical) that motherhood is now the only route to fulfilment. Unsurprisingly, Nicole and I are regarded by the Rexes of this world as creatures defying nature for daring to compete with men. To them we are figures of suspicion.

Rather less convincingly, I've had no time to contact my mother, as I've been bonding with the cats. OK, so this is utter rubbish, because I loathe them and they know it, but I have until Saturday before Dylan returns from his retreat to reclaim them. I am the first to acknowledge that bonding is too concrete a term for what has been happening, but it seems vital to envisage tasks of substance. In this mental video, I see myself seated at the piano, one cat on my lap, the other dozing at my feet whilst I play: a picture of contentment and, above all, obedience.

The prospect of Dylan's presence in my house provides my final delaying tactic, the mission of feeding him. It's essential, if one is to escape censure from the invisible judge hovering all one's life at one's shoulder, not simply to be occupied, but to be *seen* to be occupied. And so the Saturday evening is planned with meticulous precision. Matt will be on duty at the hospital, overdosing on microwaved pizza; Camp David is hosting a summit with Caryl, who wants a divorce. And Dylan and I will be alone. Plenty of time to talk.

*

The sound of cats bounding up the stairs, their nails catching on the sisal, announces Dylan's arrival.

'I suppose it was too much to hope you'd get a takeaway?' he says, following me down into the kitchen.

Yes, thank you, my father's funeral was fine, I think. My eyes fill with water, which I wipe away with my sleeve. 'And what's wrong with my cooking?' is what I actually say.

'Bambi, darling, you know I adore your little meals, and they're very worthy and nutritious. But if God hadn't meant us to eat junk food, he wouldn't have invented McDonald's.'

'He didn't,' I snap. I hate it when Dylan calls me Bambi. I know he means it sweetly, and it's part of that whole ponytail thing I had at university, but I always think it makes me sound weak and abandoned.

'He did. It's called temptation. *Deliver us from evil, and lead us not into McDonald's.* My mother couldn't spear an olive, and it hasn't done me any harm.' He loops his arms around my waist.

'And how *is* Pamela?' I ask, pouring another Pamela-sized glass of wine into the risotto.

Dylan groans. 'Mother's obsessed with this forthcoming production of *Company* in my church hall. I rue the day I ever mentioned it. She's demanding the part of Joanne.' He sneezes.

'Which one is Joanne?'

'The older alcoholic, which you have to admit is typecasting! God, how much garlic have you put in that food?' demands Dylan, sneezing again.

'None, Nigella.' I hand Dylan a box of tissues.

'Why don't you audition?'

'I haven't got time.'

'It'll take one evening.'

'Not the audition, the whole thing – rehearsals, learning the lines—'

'But Bambs, I need ballast. She keeps going through that whole *Oh, I know the perfect song to sing at the audition* theatrical thing she does, raking her hair, standing in ballet position one. And when I try to explain that it wouldn't look good if the vicar's mother gets one of the leads (like anyone would care, but I'm not going to tell *her* that), she puts on her wounded act, her *I can't believe a son would do this to his own mother* tone—'

I ask Dylan to pass me the bowls in the oven. He sneezes again, so I get them myself.

'Did the retreat fill you with special Holy Spirit,' I ask, 'or have you got the 'flu?'

'I don't know. I felt fine down in Cornwall. The sun shone, and we had some terrific discussions. Especially about the whole gays in the Church thing. Maybe it's being back in London.' He sneezes once more, and peers into the saucepan. 'You haven't used any dairy products in this, have you?'

'No,' I smile sweetly. 'Just cat meat.'

*

Two bowls scraped clean lie abandoned on the carpet. Candles flicker, casting St Vitus's dance shadows on the floor-to-ceiling bookshelves, the spines lined alphabetically. The cats have draped themselves over Dylan on the sofa. Watching them and their easy camaraderie, I am filled with a nameless dread. If only I could be sure that this whole Adoption issue was a joke. I'm on the point of broaching the subject when Dylan nudges the cats off his chest, rummages in his *baise-en-ville* and brings out a small plastic bag of weed.

'Don't look so *pi* at me, darling,' he says, rolling his eyes. 'You should see us at all-night vigils. The PCC is planning to remove all the toilet cistern tops in the church hall next week.'

I look on as he rolls the joint, and angles his smoke away from me.

'Did you know', he continues, 'that every year, vicars in villages in the south of France are presented with the best sheep of the flock?—'

There's an odd tone to Dylan's voice, and I can't quite pin it down. Then my heart starts to pound. He's emigrating to France, I think. I've pushed him away. 'France,' I say casually, as though considering the name of a popular mutual friend I secretly loathe.

'—and I was thinking how marvellous it must be to be part of a community where one is really respected. Where tradition counts for something.'

Now I think of it, Dylan sounds sad. He really *must* be thinking of moving to France.

'So, receiving farm animals is the new barometer of self-worth? What's brought this on?'

'Oh, I'm always down after retreats. Everyone's open, there's no pretence. I'm on a spiritual high. And then I come back to so-called cosmopolitan London with a bloody great bump. And I have to pretend to be something I'm not.'

'You mean, concealing the fact that you're gay?' I laugh. 'As if no one could tell!'

Dylan looks peeved. 'As I've told you before, I'm discreet. The church has, until now, favoured discretion.' He takes another long drag on his joint. 'But anyway, it looks like I won't be able to hide for much longer.' I frown. 'I should've known as soon as the press jumped on the queer-bashing bandwagon over the ordination of gay bishops that I'd have to watch my back.'

'What do you mean? I thought the media was quite accepting nowadays.'

'Simon's crawled out from under his stone. Claims he's sold his story to a tabloid.'

My eyes widen at this compelling hearsay. 'Good grief ! Simon? Why?'

'Because as we know, he is prurient.'

'Yes, but what I mean is, why now?'

'Because, Simon's not a property developer for nothing. He always could spot a good commercial opportunity when he saw one. After all, what could be more lucrative, not to say topical, than an interview with the ex-lover of a gay vicar. One practising in smart hermetically sealed Chelsea, no less.'

'But your parish isn't in Chelsea,' I snort. 'It's in one of the poorest bits of South London!'

'That's not what it's going to say in the *News of the World*, is it? When this gets out, I'll be a laughing stock.'

'You mean, if this gets out, you'll be out of a job!'

Dylan crushes his joint into his bowl, where it sizzles feebly. 'By then, I'll have ceased to care. I'm fed up with the straitjacket – no pun intended. I've known some two-faced Christians in my time, who think it's OK to be pleasant to your face and lethal behind your back, but living like this is wretched.'

'You would care,' I murmur. 'You love your job. It's just your bishop you hate.'

'I know,' Dylan sighs. 'I heard him on the radio this morning, pontificating in the God slot about the shameful practice of gays buying babies in from abroad. Christ, it makes me want to scream. *God is love*? The man doesn't know the meaning of the phrase.'

'So, I imagine, given the current climate, you and David have given up thoughts of adopting?' I tip my head to one side, trying to construct an expression of compassion.

Dylan closes his eyes and beams. 'Ah, David. I'm so lucky to have found him.' His eyes spring open. 'The question is, what did you think of him? I never had time to ask you after your dinner, what with the retreat and everything.'

Ignoring the slight jealous rumple to my equilibrium, I pretend to consider the question as though for the first time. David is older, the father Dylan never had. Yet everything about him seems unfeasibly brand-new and shiny, a performance consistent with his successful career as a rebranding consultant. He mimes quotation marks when speaking certain words; he wears silk khaki cargo pants; he shops, I suspect, at Conran. The question, I realise, is how to lie to Dylan convincingly.

'David is someone I admire,' adds Dylan, before I can commit perjury. 'He leaves a wife of thirteen years to be true to himself. That takes courage. He's not afraid to be ridiculed for what some might call a midlife crisis. He's sexy, and funny, and bright, and kind, and I adore him. Above all, he's got integrity.' The beatification of St David now complete, Dylan leans back with his arms clasped behind his skull. 'Oh, and he really likes you, by the way. That's almost the most important thing. That he should love you as much as I do.'

Can I trust that there can ever be enough love to go round?

*

It's a familiar enough scene. A man and a woman, standing at the sink at the end of an evening. One washes, the other dries. One rabbits on about babies, the needs of small children, the importance of stable families, the thrill of shopping for tiny clothes. The other listens cautiously, afraid to hear too much, practising in their head attempts to change the subject. One recounts an amusing introductory meeting where they met couples who have already adopted, and some who plan to, to learn what might be involved. How plans for the next few months must accommodate home visits from social workers, and questionnaires, and lengthy chats with family and friends.

And all this time the other is, without realising it, holding their breath, terrified that all this talk of procreation-by-proxy will dismantle the barriers they have worked so hard to keep in place – internal barriers erected long ago to keep out unresolved conflict – terrified that, once the barriers are down, all the years of unexplored longing will explode, and herald personal disintegration.

Chapter Eleven

I WAKE AT NINE. An easterly wind wafts faint chimes from Big Ben through the open window. Matt crawled into bed an hour ago, having spent the night assisting nursing staff in restraining a violent patient attempting to abscond, and cajoling another with a paranoia that the carpets harbour spies to emerge from her locked bathroom. We sift through the Sunday papers with, I am ashamed to admit, mounting excitement, only to discover that Simon's treachery has been universally usurped by a compelling exclusive of celebrity infidelity.

At three-thirty, I arrive at Ed and Louisa's. The invitation has been in the diary for weeks – a barbecue on their Tuscan stone patio overlooking one of London's smartest squares; an opportunity for Ed to grill meat and refute the myth that he is only dating Louisa for her skills as in-house cook at his investment bank.

Ed will not now, of course, be present, having moved in with his secretary. Ed is another of my university coterie. Over time, our shared experiences (lectures, parties, hangover cures) have proved more durable than Ed's manifold dalliances. These were often so short-lived that I noted each woman's passing with no more enthusiasm than I would had she been a tree glimpsed at speed from one of Ed's sports cars.

In his break-up with Louisa, I am torn. Perhaps it's inevitable that at times of crisis women feel mobilised to show solidarity, to critique the sexes and find men wanting. Hadn't we, *the girls*, dis-invited the boys, replaced the barbecue with scones and éclairs, to offer Louisa our unstinting support? But I don't want to spend the afternoon belittling men. Gatherings of women make me wary.

And yet, while not wishing to diminish the trauma of Louisa's own predicament, I have found Ed's vanishing act unsettling. When Louisa telephoned with the news of her pregnancy (requesting a lift to the twins' birthday party), I felt suddenly cold all over. And, after that call, I noticed I'd covered my blotter with doodles of three-dimensional boxes.

'Did you know your skirt's covered in cat fur, yaar?'

'Bloody Dylan's apparently allergic to the cats, so we're lumbered with them. And no, Nicole, it's not funny. Hello, I'm Amber.'

'Please, call me Prue.' The middle-aged woman now shaking my hand has the alert features of a lioness listening for the local pack of wild dogs.

'What's in the tin, Amber?' someone asks me. I've made dairy-free cheesecake. Prue says she'll fetch a plate from the kitchen. I sit down on an uncomfortable slatted-wood lounger.

'How are you feeling, Louisa?'

'Not too bad, thank you,' replies a high voice strained through tight lips, 'I haven't been sick at all today.' Louisa's green eyes seem larger, more naive than ever, her face gaunt; a portrait of grief and catastrophe covered with a light foundation of resignation.

'We were talking babies' names before you arrived,' says Jenny, hovering near the butler's table and stroking a bead-edged jug-cover. The patio is a furnace (the clipped shrubbery provides only a bonsai level of shade), and I swear Jenny is wearing her thickest sweater. If my cleavage was as fabulous as hers, I'd let everyone see it.

'Oh, great,' I say, briskly. 'I love the whole business of choosing names.' Nicole smiles, and mouths the word 'spreadsheet' at me. 'Do you know yet whether you're having a boy or a girl?' I believe it sensible to eliminate half the choices.

'Not yet. We thought—, that is—, I—, no *we* had decided not to find out,' Louisa suddenly leans forward, her eyes straining out of their sockets, 'but I was thinking that maybe, if I did find out, and managed to get hold of Eddie and told him, it might make him more responsive, you see, if he could actually visualise a boy, say, rather than a girl. And then he, you see, he might—' Her voice tails off as her mother approaches armed with a large china plate in one hand and a cake knife in the other.

'Well,' I say brightly, 'what names are on your shortlist?'

Wilting in the heat, Louisa hands me a slim paperback, before sinking back into her chair and closing her eyes. Several pages are marked with slips of paper. I steal a glance at Nicole, whose wide-eyed nod confirms that the afternoon has indeed been as stilted as it feels. I open the book at random and see that 'Merlin' has been highlighted in pink. *Ye-gods*, as Nicole would say. *No wonder Ed absconded.*

'Who's for cheesecake?' asks Prue.

'Names are so important,' says Nicole, accepting a plate and pastry fork. 'At school, there were four Janes in my class. I thought that was so boring.'

'I used to be called Jane,' says Jenny slowly, mopping up digestive biscuit crumbs with her middle finger. Everyone turns to look at her; Nicole slips me a quick grimace. 'Hmmmm. Yes,' Jenny continues, putting her finger in her mouth.

'When was this?' I say.

'University,' Jenny replies, sucking every last crumb. 'Just before I met you. I wrote "Jenny" on all the application forms. I didn't tell

71

my parents, and they never knew because all the correspondence came addressed to Miss J. Peel.'

'I never knew that,' says Nicole solemnly, helping herself quickly to another slice of cheesecake.

'No reason why you should. By the time Clive and I got married, I'd changed it legally, so even the invitations— my parents were furious about that—'

'Achha,' says Nicole, concentrating on her food.

'No, Nicole, you're right. Jane's a dull name. Plain. It shows a distinct lack of imagination. That's what I said when my parents found out, when I had to introduce them to Clive and couldn't pretend any longer. That's what I used to be called at school, you see – "Plain Jane". And when you're as large as me, you can't afford to hand your friends such easy ammunition. And I'd always thought the name Jenny sounded much more fun, much more sprightly. Like Jenny Wren, a tiny thing. I've always wanted to be small enough not to be noticed.' Her smile is tight. 'I guess it shows I've always been trying to turn myself into something else, something I'm not.' And she goes over to the table and helps herself to an éclair.

I can't move, a paralysis that makes my body burn with shame; that after Jenny's candour I seem incapable of offering her any visible support. The dry Tuscan stone between us seems too vast, too inhospitable to cross. My negligence appals me. I feel as though I might be bleeding inside.

I steal a quick glance at the other faces. None betray the turmoil I feel. Some are nodding, as if to say, *A change of name – yes, fascinating*. They don't appear to have heard what I heard: a tale of early hurts and hidden wounds. But I've heard it, and yet I sit here, rigid, helpless. I feel anger towards Jenny's parents, and hatred towards

Jenny's schoolfriends, and I say nothing, do nothing at all. Jenny reaches for another éclair. Guilt burns my gut.

And I make a decision, there and then, to reach out to others; to put 'you' before 'I' in my dealings with the world. To improve myself. I must start immediately.

'You have a very unusual name, Amber,' says Prue, gracefully. With the focus abruptly on me, I have a memory of arriving at a child's party in a velvet dress to find all the popular girls wearing jeans. 'Is it your birthstone? Are you named after that?' enquires Prue. I find myself looking into a pair of eyes similar to Louisa's, verdigris in colour.

'No,' I say, cautiously, unaware that amber is a birthstone, sensing a trap. 'I'm named after my mother's mother's ring.' I stop speaking, but no one says anything. Maybe they expect something more, a story perhaps of love and happiness, hopeful and life-affirming; where commitments were made and never broken. But I have nothing cheerful to add. I've never seen the ring, or even had it described to me – my mother's parents died in an air raid during the war. Friends at school were named after favourite relatives, or film stars, or places where they'd been 'made'; names with substance, and fond memories. When I asked my mother for stories about the ring, I was told it had gone the way of everything else, whatever that meant. And the shutters had come down.

'A ring,' says Prue, thoughtfully. 'Obviously a very precious piece of jewellery.'

I feel overwhelmed, as though by a wave of Louisa's morning sickness. And I'm convinced it will do me no good to appear vulnerable to these women. I feel a fraud, and look over at Jenny again, who is stacking plates. The doorbell sounds.

'That'll be Serena and the girls,' says Louisa, heaving herself up from her lounger. 'Can someone let them in? I'm feeling a bit peaky. Think I'll go and have a lie-down.'

*

After an hour, once Esme had fallen and gashed her knee on the Tuscan stone and the other girls had overdosed on sugar, Serena removes them from the cramped patio, leaving behind her fondest love for Louisa, who has yet to reappear. Since Jenny slipped away after answering the door to Serena, and Nicole left to see a film with Dominic, only Prue and I remain, clearing up the debris. We chat while we wash and dry, laughing at Ed's failure to install a dishwasher in his chrome kitchen. Then we take mugs of coffee on to the patio. Before sitting on one of the chairs, Prue removes the cardigan from around her shoulders, folds it into a cushion and places it on the wooden slats.

'Good idea!' I laugh.

'Stupid things. Why buy hard chairs? Just because they're in vogue. Typical, shallow Ed.'

I hesitate. Have I just been given permission? 'Has he been in touch?'

'He wouldn't dare!' says Prue. 'Not while I'm around.'

'So what's going to happen?'

'He's gifting her this flat. Buying her off, if you will. I'll stay until she's settled. Then I'll head back home. The man's a rake, and she's better off without him.'

'All the same—'

'And don't worry about Louisa hearing: she knows what her family thinks. But we'll be there for her. It's tough being a single mum. I should know – I was one when I had my first, John. I think I spent

74

his first year crying. And even in the seventies, the stigma was terrible. But I'd see his smile and know I'd done the right thing. And then I met Louisa's father, and he took us both on. Which even now I think was brave! And then Louisa came along. She'll be fine; she doesn't need Ed.' Prue drains the contents of her mug into a potted box hedge. 'Or his revolting, overpriced Fair Trade coffee. How come you're friends with such a shit?' The crows-feet at Prue's eyes disappear as she raises her eyebrows.

I explain about meeting Ed during Freshers' Week, and how by Christmas he'd single-handedly raised the money for the musical I'd performed in the following term.

'Pity Ed couldn't be the responsible type when it came to Louisa. And when are *you* going to have children?'

I choke on my mouthful of coffee.

'The little girls here earlier clearly adore you.'

I cough. 'Eloise is one of my goddaughters.'

'And you were the only one not to be annoyed by their unruly behaviour, apart from that sedated bovine mother of theirs.'

'They're just being children.'

'Yet you don't fancy having any of your own?'

How am I having this conversation with this woman? Suppose Matt and I have been trying to conceive for years? Supposing IVF has left us bereft and broken-hearted? 'Well, it's not like I'm avoiding motherhood,' I say, slightly unnerved to be saying this to a stranger. 'But it's the way of the world today; my friends are my family—'

'To me a woman isn't complete until she's had a baby.'

No one has ever spoken to me so bluntly about this subject. The weight of Prue's words bruises my skin. I have the dizzying sense that I'm staring into the abyss, that my future happiness hangs in the balance.

'Parenting gives your life meaning, and direction.'

'My life has that already,' I reply, stiffly. It occurs to me that what attracted Louisa to Ed was the echo of her mother's plain speaking. You don't get to be head of an internationally successful trading desk by being the diplomatic type.

'Yes,' says Prue. Her tone is noticeably softer now, as if she recognises belatedly that I'm not the person she wishes to reprimand. 'Being a mother's hard work. And many's the time I'd be shouting at the children – although usually John, because Louisa was such a good baby – and I'd think, *What have I done to deserve this? You are an unspeakably horrible little child and I wish I'd never had you!*'

'You used to say that?' A memory stirs in my mind.

'Only in my head!' Prue laughs. 'But sometimes that was enough. To give myself permission to contemplate those words. They were my escape.'

'My mother said that to me once. On a beach.'

Prue looks doubtful.

I rush to say, 'I don't know. There are so many things I want to do before having a baby.'

'It doesn't mean the end of your life. I went back to studying.'

'What did you read?' I ask, quickly.

'It was all Louisa's father's idea; I left university when John came along. I did an Open University degree in Psychology and now I'm a clinical psychologist for the parole board.'

That, I say to myself, *would explain your forensic interrogation skills.* 'So you had a complete career change.'

'No,' says Prue, glancing back towards the flat. 'You never stop being a mother.'

On the way out, we look in on Louisa, lying asleep on top of the duvet, her swollen belly the focal point in the room, drawing the eye, like a foetus siphoning off all the nutrients. Louisa appears grave, which to me suggests that even in sleep she recognises how narrow her life has become; that she's already acquainted with limitation.

'It was very nice of you all to make the effort to come,' whispers Prue on the doorstep. 'Please thank your friends for me. I know my daughter appreciated it.'

'Oh, it was nothing, it was our pleasure.'

'No, Amber, it was a big thing. You are good friends of Ed's, and I'm sorry you've all been put in this awkward position.'

'We can do so little. She's lucky to have *you*.'

'Oh, I'm just doing what any mother would do.'

*

Out in the street, I experience an abrupt rush of giddiness. I double over, almost retching, as I cling to a nearby garden wall. My chest feels punctured as if no amount of air would ever be sufficient to fill my lungs. How has this happened, this rupture? Why this feeling of melancholy – of envy, no less! For what? The promise of congratulations cards and bouquets? Contact from people who read birth announcements and use them as an excuse to resurrect obsolete friendships?

I long to believe in the potential for fulfilment, that one tiny seed can offer redemption. But right now I can't say that I do. Louisa and Prue's relationship feels unfamiliar to me, as does their trust in the redeeming power of maternal love. And it is this lack of connection that so unnerves me.

*

Initially, I don't tell Matt about my chat with Prue. Instead, I ask about his afternoon watching a televised Grand Prix.

'A procession,' he scoffs, with rare irritation. I envy the way Matt is able to confine his conflicts to sport. But then containment is his stock in trade.

You should see him with his fellow sports fiends such as Peder, shouting at the television, or providing running commentaries on what should be happening on the pitch, or on court, or in the pit, or on the green, or at fine leg. A sporting event without competition is, for Matt, barren and pointless. The most enjoyable contests are those with something at stake. And once the match, the race, the tournament is over, it's as though his emotions have been properly digested.

Matt has asked me once or twice why I prefer my sport to be so predictable. And I snap that there is perhaps too much conflict in the world, which is unfair. As a white child of apartheid, crunching on racial eggshells, Matt knows all about conflict. Twenty years ago, on finishing at his English boarding school, he returned to South Africa to do his national service and found himself, at the age of eighteen, with an R4 rifle in his hand, patrolling the border with southern Angola. Doing his bit to keep his nation safe. You don't need to lecture a man who has come across the remains of a former comrade sliced in half about conflict.

I lie on the sofa, in his arms. Through the open French windows I can see that the late August sky is marbled with the crinkly thin strata of bruise-coloured clouds. After several tracks of a CD, he asks if I'm all right.

I hold his gaze. I want to ask him something; want to ask him not because I'm curious as to the answer, but because I need him to cro-

chet a security blanket of neat rows of reasons. To hear him recount
how we adore our life; how we enjoy being able to travel at a
moment's notice (hospital rotas permitting), eating out, seeing the
latest films and musicals, and discussing them with friends over late
dinners. Sometimes on holiday we observe parents with a new baby,
glimpse something of this couple's shared joy at opening up the
world for their child, and we smile at each other, with a look as if to
say *We could, you know. Why don't we?* And a foul infant, screaming
on the return flight home, answers that question for us.

I wonder whether to tell him what I did in the taxi. How I
breathed a pool of condensation on to the window, and drew a tiny
heart shape, and then parts of an arrow poking out the sides. How
at one end of the arrow I used a fingernail to etch Matt's initials, and
at the other end my own. Yes, Matt was the kind of man whose
name I would have scratched on my locker had I known him at
school. He would have toyed with my teenage heart, tossing it aside
like chewed gum, confirming my belief that love is finite. But now?
Now he's the man into whose hands my father transferred me for
safekeeping, who holds my heart together – an undertaking of such
importance, such delicacy, it renders me incapable of disturbing its
equilibrium.

And yet, and yet.

Just lately I've been grappling (what with Dylan's plan to adopt,
and Harry's wish for a son) with how Matt feels about eschewing
parenthood. Or, more specifically, with whether he might ever
change his mind. In my head I weigh each possibility. Sadness –
arguments – divorce? It's easy to remember the heady moment
when he said he wanted to marry me, and to forget that just before
that he'd referred to a different life, with a different woman and a
whole rugby team of children. And it sometimes occurs to me that,

while Matt might never have really thought about having children, this might also mean that he never gave much thought to *not* having children. And when I think about that, and about the sacrifice he made for me, the dreams he might have laid to one side, I break out into vicious cold sweats, and I find myself reaching increasingly often for the hair at my parting, to feel the small stabs of pain on my scalp.

Through the French windows, the evening air hangs heavy and still, hinting at the forecast storm; Mother Nature is holding her breath. Maybe, I think, I should ask my question, to rid myself of its toxicity and relieve the pounding in my head.

I met a woman today, I want to say, who hinted at knowing the meaning of life. Who mentioned it so matter-of-factly that it had to be true. I can be seduced by clarity, I want to remind my husband. I read fiction, and recipe books; I need music, I cannot play the piano by ear. I also like to earn the approval of others. If I thought the route suggested by this woman offered me universal approbation, I would embrace it wholeheartedly. But I am consumed with doubt. I mistrust the information.

Am I brave enough, I wonder, to have a change of heart?

The source of my conflict is a fear that Prue may be right. That in avoiding babies I've made an error of judgement. I've built my life on the foundation of not wanting babies. It was never my plan to equivocate. Yet now my confidence is shaken. Maybe a woman's life without children is like a sporting event without competition: barren and pointless. Maybe there needs to be more at stake.

So, if I ask you my question, dear husband, it's not because I want you, in your masculine way, to fix things, or to reveal to me that you've changed your mind, or to dissect the choices I've made, but to have you sense the subtext in all of this, and simply stop the world imploding.

Chapter Twelve

'SO, HOW WAS IT?'

Nicole and I sit on benches overlooking the river, escaping a conference on corporate governance. We nibble sandwiches, and comment on the cloudy sky. The Thames flows as brown as milky coffee, foaming in the wash as if stirred with an invisible spoon.

'Dull, yaar,' answers Nicole, peeling back bread to inspect the filling. 'But then I find film sequels usually are. Did Louisa resurface?' I shake my head. 'Weird how she left just as Serena and the kids arrived.'

'And you, in her condition, would have stayed?' I ask. 'I think not.'

'True, but then I'm not pregnant. I assumed Louisa liked children.'

'Me, too. Why else go through pregnancy?'

'Perhaps she felt she had no choice.'

'C'mon. Women today are free to choose anything.'

'Absolutely. But for some, freedom is slavery,' says Nicole, pushing her greaseproof parcel of uneaten food to one side.

'I reckon that was just Orwell being typically cryptic. As a misogynist, he refused to endorse the idea of liberating women.'

'Orwell was a misogynist?'

'Sure,' I say, hurriedly, screwing up my sandwich wrapping into a tight ball. 'He was firing a warning shot across the early feminists' bows, saying, *Don't imagine you can ever be totally free*, meaning free of *men*. You are familiar with the sentiment. Dominic tolerates your brain and ambition, but secretly he just wants to look after you. And you pander to his delusions by letting him pay for things like yesterday's cinema tickets.'

'I pander to Dominic, yaar,' says Nicole with a smile, 'because it suits my purpose to have my traditional, Rajput family think I'm about to marry and have kids. You can't imagine the shame my grandmother inflicts on my papa for having an unmarried daughter. Why do you think I haven't been back to Delhi in, what, three years?'

Pigeons approach the crumbs at our feet, sense the lethal kick waiting in my shoe, and think better of it. 'But women like us have *all* the choices. We've drunk from the cup of emancipation. We've chosen not to become parents. It's the women having babies who've limited their options.' An image of Prue pops into my mind, and I try to block her out.

'Absolutely,' says Nicole, sipping mineral water. 'Some women have babies when they've run out of things to do. Take that girl I had temping for me recently. She'd been to university, bright, capable. No ambition. Spoke of having a baby as if she was choosing a holiday.'

'Which proves it's still about choice. To insist I have no choice is to say I choose not to take responsibility.'

Nicole sighs. 'What about the ones who can't choose? Couples who are infertile? There's a big difference between choosing not to have children and being told you can't.'

I pick at the filling of Nicole's abandoned sandwich. 'Mother Nature is a law unto herself.'

'So, by choosing not to become pregnant, we're winning the battle for our lives.'

'Ah, but who do we imagine we are fighting?'

A woman and her two daughters, their hair in tight cornrows, join the queue for the London Eye. The girls are singing playground songs, about the important things in life, like kissing and boys' names. With a spasm in my stomach I recall the familiar rhymes, and the constant dread of being the one frozen out of playtime games.

My mother said I never should play with the gypsies in the wood
If I did, she would say, 'naughty little girl to disobey ...'

Have the choices I've made, I wonder as I lick my fingers, been defined by this impulse to escape the snare, and revolt? To disobey?

*

'Have you, or has anyone you know, ever been affected by premature births?'

Unable to endure further lectures (or rather to escape the Churchill Conference Suite, which has the kind of arctic air-conditioning system that paralyses your eyeballs), we are queuing for the London Eye. A young woman with a clipboard has been working her way down the line. We watch two men ahead of us dismiss her with a wave of the hand.

She is conducting research for a local neonatal unit. Do we realise that around ten per cent of the babies born in Britain need some kind of special care at birth? Are we aware of the various medical conditions contributing to early labour? Could we look at these pictures of premature babies wired up to machines? I peer over Nicole's shoulder, and see that their fists are no bigger than coins. My whole face tingles as tears spring to my eyes.

And I have a sudden memory of my mother and me, watching an

item on *Nationwide* about premature babies. When they showed one in an incubator, my mother leaped to the screen with a shriek, switched off the set and sent me straight to bed.

Afterwards, the girl with the clipboard thanks us for our time, before moving on.

'I think I've just had my maternal moment, yaah,' says Nicole, placing the folded Gift Aid form in her handbag, before retrieving a hairbrush.

'You know that girl was hoping to appeal to our maternal side.'

'Absolutely.'

By now we are snaking up the ramp towards the Ferris wheel. I can't wait to be inside our warm pod – equal ovals, rotating in an endless, graceful circle, which I find rather soothing.

But questions continue to buzz round my head. 'Why do you think a woman choosing not to have a baby is still such a taboo?'

'Because it shows she's inherently evil and deserves to be burned at the stake.'

'I'm serious, Nics. Nobody bats an eyelid when children are sent to boarding school at seven, or spend their childhood being cared for by a succession of nannies and au pairs.'

'Ayaah!' she laughs. 'That's the *acceptable* face of not wanting kids. There are women out there who wish they'd never had them. Not that they want to kill their own children, no one is suggesting infanticide here. It's just that they suspect their lives would be less stressful if their children belonged to someone else, someone they could visit on a regular basis. Or not. But the taboo's so powerful, we can't even acknowledge that it exists as a taboo.'

'So, why's that?'

'Because women who don't want a baby are, by definition, empty specimens. Nature abhors a vacuum.'

I snort. 'And all people with children are by definition kind and unconditionally loving? I must remember that when I next bump into Ed.'

Our pod glides into position. Nicole turns to me. 'Well, by fathering a child, Ed is deemed by society to have given something back. Reimbursement for his very existence. Now he'll have permission to carry on living.'

We step inside. I stand gazing out over the river with my hands in my pockets. 'I think that not enough women today believe they have permission *not* to have them.'

*

Our pod hovers near the top of the wheel. The afternoon sun casts its rays over London, which appear as shimmering fishing rods from behind a bank of dark rain clouds.

'So, you think women are still trapped by their fertility?' says Nicole, who sits down on the central bench to counter an unexpected lurch of vertigo.

'I'm saying that many imagine themselves to be, yes.' I turn to her. 'We make excuses for not going it alone, we say we lack the opportunity. We are the generation which has read *A Room of One's Own*, which now has access to one, and yet still finds the world wanting.'

Nicole nods. 'We lack a vision of our potential.'

'Some see it,' I say, brightly. 'A woman co-designed this wheel. I know nothing more about her, but her imagination was audacious. I admire her for that.'

'So, what did you mean back there, when you said that some women feel trapped?'

'I mean that women are expected to have babies, and that, for some, that expectation is too mighty, too ingrained to oppose. We've come so far, yet we must conform; must turn ourselves into something we're not. Or reject the role allotted to us, and be punished.'

'Or pitied.'

'Or envied.' I pause, remembering my mother, the time I won my place at university, asking me what was wrong with taking up a permanent job with Marks and Spencer.

*

My steps have slowed. 'Have you ever thought that you and I might be wrong about all this?' I ask, as we walk towards Westminster Bridge to find a cab.

'Achha, no!' cries Nicole. 'What on earth makes you say that?'

'Just something Louisa's mother said.'

'She wanted to know why we haven't had kids?'

'Not us. Me.'

'Ye-gods! I hope you put her straight.'

I did try, I want to say, blinking into the glare that Nicole's statement has shone on my deficiencies.

Pillowy clouds race across the sky, late for an appointment. Tourists jostle us, pointing their phones with outstretched arms towards the Houses of Parliament. I marvel, mildly, at their sense of purpose. And in that instant I know that I can't put off a meeting with my mother any longer. The orange beacon of an empty taxi appears over the brow of Westminster Bridge. I raise my arm; it feels unbelievably heavy.

As we hurtle round the one-way system of Vauxhall Cross, we pass a crowd of people aiming for the station. In the blur of faces and bodies I am stabbed by the sense that I have just glimpsed my mother. Hair, build, posture: in that second, they are the random pieces of some absurdly perfect Photofit. Each fragment has the potential to be what I want this person to be: Mum, confidante, friend; someone to stop the cab for, and rush over to embrace. The words crackle in my head, creating jump-lead sparks to my heart. And then we are gone – the cab has turned the corner, and the woman, this construct, has disappeared from view.

I can still see her.

I always see her.

Chapter Thirteen

MY NECK is stiff from gazing up at the statues around the gallery courtyard balustrade. I've come for stimulation, to absorb from these masters something of the creative impulse. The business pitch is three days away, and I've yet to complete a shortlist of candidates. I need to concentrate. For two years running I've billed the highest number of revenues worldwide. Now I'm distracted, my days consumed by the single thought that I must meet my mother.

When I dare to imagine this visit, my mind lacks focus. It's not that I am unable to recall where my mother now lives, or how she might look. A woman who has had the same Joan of Arc bob for forty years is unlikely to have embraced change since I last saw her, at my wedding three years ago. Rather, my mind is paralysed by dread. And when stray memories do penetrate the blur, all scrupulous attempts at self-preservation disintegrate, and I become weary, and snappy, and tearful.

Sitting on a courtyard step, I recall the grey of a deserted pebble beach. My family, that holy trinity, has come to a remote scar of coastline, eschewing the penny arcades and greasy chip papers of Bognor Regis that Mother finds so repugnant. The wind blows, as it always does. Cue Mother berating Dad for failing yet again to pack the windbreak. I am now properly out of nappies. Which is a shame, as their extra padding might have made the shingle more comfortable.

Dad is finding all the funny-looking stones, turning them over in his hands. I sit beside him, listening to the stories he tells. He shows me what he can see in the pebbles. This one's the shoe that housed so many children; this round one is the apple eaten by Snow White. It's just like when he lets me help him make things out of clay. Or when he reads me *Winnie-the-Pooh* at bedtime. I know all the Winnie-the-Pooh stories off by heart. I always know when my mother is missing out bits.

My favourite stones are the ones as large as Dad's fist. These are elephants, he says, or well-fed mice. He invites me to stroke their backs. These I place in a pile to one side, to be taken home and stroked in secret. Did I know, he asks, that this particular elephant swam to Sussex all the way from India? India, he tells me, is very far away. The elephant was so hot he needed to cool down, and so he dived into the water in Bombay. Once he was in, he splashed around and sprayed water over his back with his trunk. He splashed, and splashed, and was enjoying himself so much he didn't realise he'd swum halfway round the world. But that was how he ended up on this beach. And this mouse thought the sea was made of blue cheese, and came down to the water to eat it all up! Silly old mouse. My dad is really funny.

Mother interrupts to say that Dad might go for his swim now before luncheon is served. Lunches on the beach are always egg sandwiches, without salad cream. Egg sandwiches without salad cream smell of poo.

I watch as Dad hops across the stones in his bare feet, turning round to wave at me, and pulling funny faces because of the stones and the cold water. The sea reaches up to his knees, and now the bottom of his baggy shorts. Then he pushes off, and he doesn't turn to wave any more. I stare at him as he gets smaller. The wind blows my hair across my face, and makes my eyes sting.

The sound of the tide over shingle roars in my ears. There is no sand on this beach – the reason my mother gives for not buying me a bucket and spade. Seagulls cry out overhead. *Yark*, I repeat. *Yark*.

'That was your first word,' says my mother, and not for the first time. She means 'bird', not the seagull's screech. So, my first word was something that flies away.

Dad likes his swims, so my mother and I both know that it'll be a while before he returns for lunch. She and I are now utterly alone, sitting side by side, on the knobbly beach. In the huge silence, the sound of the wind is very loud in my ears.

'I know,' announces my mother. 'Let's play ducks' tails.'

I've never heard of the game.

'We throw stones into the water so that they bounce on the waves, and we count how many bounces the stone makes before sinking. That will tell us how many ducks' tails there are.'

This doesn't quite make sense to me, and I feel bad that I haven't understood.

Picking up some stones, Mother places them in her sunhat and strides off towards the water's edge. I follow, staring at my feet in their scuffed red sandals, unsteady on the pebbles. Once, I nearly fall over, so I stop and look up in case my mother wants to help me. Instead, I see that she's already at the water's edge, leaning back into a throw, her right arm extended on a level with her hip. Then, with a twist of her elbow and a whip of her wrist, she sends the stone flying out across the sea. Even before I reach her, I know what's wrong. The grey stones being thrown are too smooth, too beautiful to be tossed away.

Mother turns. 'That one made four bounces. How many do you

think this one will make?' In her powerful grip she holds up the elephant that swam all the way from India.

'No,' I blurt out.

Mother hesitates, looking down at me with that scary stare of hers. 'What on earth do you mean, "No"?'

'No,' I say again, quietly, more like a whimper, for my mother's stares are often enough to make even my dad leave a room. I start to cry, my hot tears splashing on to my sandals.

'You', snaps my mother, 'are an unspeakably selfish little girl, and I wish I'd never had you! Just because you're not big enough to throw stones, there's no need to throw a tantrum instead.'

I stand wobbling on the pebbles. I cannot speak. My eyes are locked on the elephant in my mother's hand. My body feels cold in the wind.

'Right,' snaps my mother, turning back to the sea. 'Play on your own. See if I care. And you can explain to your father why you were crying over nothing.' And, as she says this, all I can do is watch the brave elephant rise high into the sky and then drop towards the sea.

*

I glance round the courtyard, but no one notices me. I dab at my eyes, blow my nose, and pick up my handbag, before striding out towards Piccadilly. I always terminate that memory at the moment the elephant stone plops beneath the waves. I *must* get back to work.

I have just switched on my computer when Maxine puts through a call.

'Got that Shields Holdings search completed yet?' a voice barks.

'I need to talk to you about that,' I say, struggling to get a word past Rex's brusque, ex-armed forces manner. 'Their CEO's landed a sexual harassment charge. Our candidate for the FD job is threatening to withdraw. It's not looking good.'

'Look, Amber. I really need— I mean, the firm really needs that fee booked by the end of this quarter. Tell the board to dump the CEO. That way, we could pick up another search—'

'I doubt it. The Chairman's defending him.'

'What on earth for?'

I drop my voice. 'The Chairman's up for three harassment charges himself.'

'Impossible,' bellows Rex. 'He played last year in my four-ball in Sotogrande—'

I sigh, and press the button to open the Venetian blinds coating the clear acrylic panels of my office. I stand and gaze out across the open-plan floor. I see Dominic take a detour to the water fountain via Nicole's office and lean incestuously in the doorway. A man who manages to look both fat and fit. Maxine and another secretary stand photocopying CVs while sharing a copy of *Heat*. A researcher is applying lipstick as a prelude to lunch in St James's Park. (*We regret to inform you of the temporary closure today of the staff canteen due to pest-control fumigation.*)

While Rex monopolises my right ear, I open an email from Dylan, inviting Matt and me to Sunday lunch. He's obviously online, because his reply to my next email is immediate.

Haven't you spoken to your mother yet?

Not as such.

My mobile rings almost immediately. I could, Dylan suggests, absolve my conscience by entertaining *his* mother instead. Pamela has been invited for lunch to be told of the adoption plans. It's the kind of *family conversation* on which the adoption agency insists.

There's a pause in which I hear Dylan give short shrift to a parishioner calling at the door for salvation – then to me, *Do come, I need your support*. His anxiety soothes me; I feel wanted. Perhaps the company of someone else's mother will provide the perfect impetus for me to visit mine.

Having said goodbye to Dylan, I turn my attention back to Rex.

'—and get Julia to send me a fax when you've done it,' he booms.

That, I think, will be impossible. Julia, in Rex's absence, is avoiding work with all the mutinous venom of a toddler refusing food.

*

'Where to, love?'

I describe in detail the route to take. I'm exhausted, and want to get home as quickly as possible. As we crawl west towards Hyde Park, the driver maintains an uninterrupted stream of consciousness, until finally I'm aware of a clunking lack of sound.

'I said, what you do, then?'

I come to and tell him, picking at a stray thread in my trousers.

'Got my CV in 'ere somewhere,' he laughs, reaching over to the glove compartment while I roll my eyes. 'Hah! Only kidding. Reckon you can get me a job?'

I explain that headhunters don't find jobs for people; rather people for jobs. Even I can hear that I sound prissy.

'Sounds like jobs for the boys to me!'

So I use the analogy of finding him a wife.

'Be my guest, darlin'. Only, do a better job than what I done last time rahnd!'

I laugh. He's growing on me. 'Well, I interview *you* to find out

94

what kind of woman you want. And then, after I've interviewed the best candidates, you meet the shortlist.'

'I like *that* bit!' He has a deliciously throaty snigger. 'So, what sort of people do you, er—'

'Place?'

'Yeah, "place".'

'I mainly do chairmen and chief executives now—'

'Very high-powered, I'm sure. Bet you're good.' There is a minute pause. 'Kids?'

My stomach contracts. The question is always there. As if it mattered. As if everything beforehand, the apparent interest in my career, the flattery, has been merely preamble.

Stuck with Blu-Tack to his dashboard are photos of two 'kids' in school uniform. The boy, no doubt yanked off the football pitch and made to sit still, sports a cowlick. The girl, older, wears a bulky cardigan, the type in which grandmothers excel. *Why did you bother having children*, I want to ask? *Where are they now, as you ferry me around on a Friday evening? When do you see them? Or are these photos to remind you they exist? What happened to your first wife? What effect did divorce have on your kids? Is your life more complete with them in it? Are your children happy?*

Or do they hate being a child as much as I did?

And now I can't stop the memory, the one I can usually freeze the moment the elephant stone sinks beneath the waves, from barging in. How, as I turn to follow my mother back up the wobbly pebbles, I step into an ice cream someone has dropped, one with a square cone and a brick of yellow ice cream like I'll be allowed to have when I'm bigger. First of all, I feel the cold ice cream on my toes. Then I feel tickling. I look down to find tiny black creatures crawling all over my feet. Ants! They run across my nails, and over my scuffed sandals. Then they are circling my ankles, and running up my leg. I scream, and stamp my feet up and down. Nothing like this has ever happened to me before, and I want it to end now. I jiggle my legs, and overbalance. And still they cling on.

Finally, I scream once more, and sense my mother turn around. The tickling on my legs is unbearable. Mother comes towards me and then stops. She will get rid of them. I gulp for air.

'Serves you right,' she says, staring at my legs. Digging her heels into the pebbles, she turns around and clambers back up the slope. I watch her hike to where a plastic Spar carrier bag sits knocking in the wind. I have forgotten the ants. All I want is for my mother to turn round and reach out her hand. She picks up a library hardback, opens it and begins to read.

Her voice, as I recall it now in the cab, contained all the triumph normally reserved for observing the painful demise of one's husband's mistress.

Chapter Fourteen

'WELL, that wasn't too awful, was it?' says David brightly, slamming the front door.

From the far end of the church cul-de-sac, Pamela's car can still be heard straining in first gear. Dylan's vicar-cage is a modest Victorian cottage near 'Colombia Common', rechristened for its popularity with drug pushers. The more narcotically desirable the area, the greater the number of car-chase-repellent road bumps. Soon Pamela's car can be heard in the distance attacking one at speed.

We return to the kitchen to wash up. Or, rather, David washes, Matt and I dry, and Dylan smokes and tells us where to put things. Dylan has never seen the need to acquire a dishwasher. That's what parishioners are for.

'I thought she was choking on a roast potato,' remarks David, as yet unused to Pamela's repertoire of voices and facial expressions. Dylan's mother lives by her wit. Unskilled, as were so many women of her class and generation in anything but marital mergers and acquisitions, she was raised to believe that her passport in life was not so much to entertain as to be entertaining. Her parents having disapproved of a career on the stage, the woman has reacted by turning every encounter into a vaudeville act, every conversation a chance for a soliloquy. Years of practice have proved constructive, for now she has a regular spot on Tuesday nights as a cable television quiz-show panellist.

'I wish she had,' mutters Dylan, in between cigarettes.

'Darling, she wants to make sure you're happy. That we're doing the right thing,' says David, depositing a baby meringue of soap suds on Dylan's nose. I want to vomit.

Dylan laughs. 'I know, I know. But even *I* was appalled by her outburst, and I've seen some in my time. She'll be off now on one of her Michael Douglas *Falling Down* rampages. Anyone would think we're planning to adopt a Siberian throat monkey. I hoped a mother whose son is gay would be more, well, tolerant.'

'She'll be fine in a day or two,' says Matt. He makes it sound as though Pamela is one of his patients. Perhaps she is!

'And it's not as though the adoption's definitely happening,' I say, attempting to sound casual. 'Is it?'

'No,' groans Dylan, hand to forehead. 'The whole plan's a night-mare. Tell them about the video, darling.' So, David describes how at one of the agency meetings they'd watched footage of a suppos-edly authentic story depicting a family destroyed by the arrival of a disturbed adolescent. 'They certainly do their best to put you off.'

'I think it's good they make you reflect,' says Matt, reaching for cups. A rare personal opinion, I observe, from my husband. I married the epitome of nonchalance, after a childhood of critical judgement. I smile, as he continues. 'It's a pity more people don't consider the effect kids will have on a relationship before they conceive.'

'You wouldn't be thinking of the lovely Louisa and Ed, would you?' smirks Dylan.

'Not especially,' Matt replies, arranging the cups on a tray. 'There are lots of unhappy children out there. Most of them are grown up, now, of course.'

I can feel my cheeks reddening, and make a point of rummaging in the fridge for the milk.

'So, isn't it up to people like us to offer a fresh start?' says David, above the rolling boil and click of the kettle. *But you've got children already*, I think.

'David, you might be right,' says Matt, lifting the tray and making for the lounge. 'But if you carry on saving broken spirits at this rate, I'll be out of a job!'

*

After evensong, Dylan and I return to the vicar-cage; Matt cries off to dictate case notes, David, to attend to lingering post-divorce matters. Around Dylan's kitchen table, he and I sip black coffee and prise apart pistachios; Dylan thinks two-syllable snacks are common.

'How are you feeling about your dad?' asks Dylan.

I manage a nod and a sort of grimace.

'It takes time,' says Dylan, crossing to a cupboard under the sink to retrieve his *baise-en-ville* from behind a tub of household cleaning products.

'This kind of thing helps,' I say.

'What? Shelling nuts with a sad homosexual? Ooh – *Will & Grace*, eat your heart out.'

'It *is* helping.' I manage to laugh. 'Don't knock it. And anyway, what's with the "sad"?' I put my mug down on the pine. 'You and David aren't splitting—?'

Dylan shakes his head.

'What, then?'

'Nothing.' He gestures at his snap-lock packet of weed. And for the first time, I seriously consider it; instead, I pull at strands of hair near my crown. I watch him roll his joint, as he explains how he lives in dread of a call from the Bishop, 'demanding a little chat, setting one of his little traps—'

'That's unlikely, surely. What sort of traps?'

'The "we've noticed you're not married yet" ones.'

'But why now? You've been in this parish, what, five years? Who'd tell tales?'

So he tells me about Peter, a vicar from another diocese, who'd accepted a new job running a church mission for the homeless, but who'd recently been leant on by the Bishop to withdraw from the post because he was actively gay.

'As if he'd *want* to stay in the church, if that's how it carries on,' I say.

'Quite. Competence is no longer the issue. Whether you're sleeping with someone of the same sex apparently is.' He takes a long drag on his spliff and exhales slowly. 'So, I'm thinking of leaving.'

I stare at him, open-mouthed. 'Leaving the church?' I swallow. 'What ever happened to faith, hope and charity?'

Somewhere deep inside I have the sensation of old scabs splitting. Not that I'm so religious that his departure could weaken my virtually nonexistent faith. But something about Dylan being untethered leaves me reeling. I lunge for his parcel of dope, and make a hash of opening it. I've watched Dylan roll joints for years, and I can't for the life of me begin to remember how he does it, so my spliff ends up very droopy.

'Ah, little Bambi-bunny,' says Dylan, offering me his lighter. 'That's the problem with the church. It still expects those of us who preach its gospels to live the life of saints. And Christianity, for lots of people around the world, means "no gays".'

I inhale quickly, as if to deny the act to myself. My heart is racing. I am taking drugs! Wa-hey! I am part of an inner circle. Stick that in your Bambi-shaped pipe and smoke it! 'I remember when there was that fuss about appointing a gay bishop—'

'Yes, but—'

'And in the States, they've got gay bishops, haven't they? So we can, too.'

''Fraid not. My stipend's paid from a national pot. If the church ordains gay bishops, wealthier, anti-gay parishes will withdraw their funding. There won't be enough money to pay priests like me, and the church will split.'

'It won't,' I scoff. 'The church has weathered rifts for centuries. There's a tithe barn in my home village, mentioned in the Domesday Book, regarding a dispute over the appointment of a rector—'

'Oh, right. So, it's OK for the church to behave as it did in the thirteenth century?'

'Well—'

'The problem is', he spits, 'that the church is confused.' He snatches another handful of his beloved pistachios. '"God is love", they say. "God will forgive you. Come to confession and be absolved of sin." Which is all very well until you're a man loving a man. Then they don't want to know. You're evil. An outcast.' He's striding around the kitchen now. 'I'd say that most of my parish know I'm gay. They accept it; they're not bothered. But there are a few, who praise my sermons and admire my fundraising abilities, who invite me to lunches to meet their eligible nieces. Now, if *they* suspected, they'd petition to have me thrown out. They'd write to Lambeth Palace, insist I was a bad influence; say I was undermining traditional biblical morality. I'm the same person who delivers the wonderful homilies, who consoles them in their grief. But the *real* me offends them.'

Even I, with my slightly doped-out brain, can hear Dylan's bitterness. I ought to be able to relate to all this, but I can't get a hold of it. My mind is scrambled.

'Look,' he continues. 'Don't get me wrong. I'm really trying to see both sides. I've got a great supervisor, and she and I talk about this every day. I have a responsibility to my parish, to my parishioners – even the ones whose views conflict with my own. I know that. All I'm saying is, I'm finding it difficult. Unbelievably difficult. I've lost sight of who I really am. And I don't know whether to renounce my sexuality for my calling, or renounce my calling for my sexual integrity. Either way, I'm buggered. As the actress said to the bishop.'

On the table lie shrivelled nuts ripped from their shells. They look naked. I start to giggle uncontrollably.

Dylan stops pacing up and down. 'It wasn't that funny— Bambi, are you stoned?'

'No,' I snigger. 'Am I?' I feel fantastic!

'Sometimes people get thirsty, especially their first time. Or hungry. Are you hungry?'

'Don't you get stoned?'

'Not so much now. Look, don't have any more, you're not used to it.' Dylan takes my joint and props it against the nut bowl.

I try to sulk, but my brain has mislaid the instructions. I sigh happily. 'I feel content. Is that part of it?'

Outside it is twilight, although the oak tree in the middle of the garden makes the kitchen seem darker. I look at Dylan carefully, this surrogate family of mine. Perhaps Dylan is in some way my mother, and Matt my father; and perhaps this is why I made the choice I did, not to have children: I'm the needy child. I feel sweaty and uncomfortable.

And yet, even as the dope wraps me in its lethargy, I sense something shifting in me. And Jenny pops into my head, along with a sense of guilt that by not reaching out to her that time on the Tuscan stone patio, I have somehow aggravated her sense of loneliness.

This is what I see tonight. That Dylan is struggling to find his path in life. He is someone who needs to be stroked. It's just that I'm unsure how to do it.

Dylan sits at the table and clasps his hands behind his head. His voice is very calm. Too calm. 'I haven't told David yet, but I *have* had The Call from the Bish. Left when I was on retreat. Wanting that chat-ette.' He spits the final consonant. 'I think we can guess what *that's* all about. So, I've got the Bish, my parish and David. And I can't say I'm handling any of them very well. Talk about a test of faith.'

I'm shouting. 'Well, you can't punish your parish? The people who need you most?'

'Oh, please. I was married to the church. Don't you get that? And every time the church hurt me, a little piece of my love for it died. Now it's nearly all gone, dried up.'

'Is that what this adoption is all about?' Even as I hear my own words, I hate myself. I decide it's the dope making me so belligerent.

'Is it connected? I honestly don't know. I wondered the other day whether I'm going along with it because it's an easier decision to make than leaving the church. There – isn't that dreadful?'

I latch on to the words *going along with it*. 'I don't understand.'

'Well, if we did go the whole way, and had a civil partnership, and adopted a child, I'd probably be sacked anyway, so then I wouldn't have to make the decision myself. God, I'm such a coward,' he adds, sinking his head into his hands.

In an odd way, it's a relief to find that someone else is struggling; Matt, of course, being the golden child, glides through this thing called life. The rest of us are stuck on the first page of its basic equations, trying our best to live up to the ideals of the world, without losing sight of who we are. And I have a flash of memory of the summer ritual in our house, which was that my mother would bake her annual cake, a project that would always fail. It wouldn't rise, or it burned to a cinder, or it stayed eggy in the middle. And she would completely erupt, and rip up the recipe, and hurl the tin in the bin, along with the cake. And every year – in June it was, which is strange because none of us had a birthday in June – she would try again with a new tin, a new recipe. And, whatever she did, the cake never turned out as it should. The smell of burned batter would linger in the house for days.

'If you ask me,' Dylan says, 'I'll be better off *with* kids. And the love I once poured into the church I can now devote to children. *My* children.'

'But what do you get? After twenty years, they walk out the door, and never come back. Not to mention the fact that they'll probably hate you by then, anyway—'

'Hate?' Dylan stares at me, puzzled.

I blush and blunder on. 'Have you really thought what having children means? You're being so selfish.'

'*I'm* being selfish?' Dylan bellows.

Oh, my God – we are arguing. I grip the edge of the table with both hands. 'You're right. Forgive me,' I beg. 'I'm the selfish one here. It must be smoking this stuff. I'm really sorry.'

Dylan reaches out for me. 'No, it's my fault. I should never have let you try it.'

In silence, we each draw small piles of shells across the table into a cupped palm. We could be no more awkward around each other than if we'd just slept together. I move to the sink, and turn on a tap. The water comes out so forcefully that the jet ricochets off a spoon and sprays the front of my clothes. Dylan lunges for a tea towel and begins dabbing at my groin.

'Dylan!' I cry in pretend disgust, and wallop him on the bottom.

'If only one of my parishioners could walk in now, I could say I ejaculated prematurely. Who'd call me gay, then?'

*

As I let myself into the house, I'm surprised to see a strip of light trimming the study door. I assumed Matt would have taken his paperwork to bed. He pulls open the study door from where he sits at his computer. 'Heyyy!' he says, softly.

'What are you doing?' I ask, after we kiss. It's comforting to think he's waited up. He takes hold of my hands and I crouch down between his knees. 'What is it?'

'One of the cats has been run over.' His grip tightens. Matt found it beside the kerb in our street, lying as though having passed out after a squalid night on the town. The animal is now decomposing in a carrier bag in the back garden. Trusting in the importance of correct procedure, Matt has been trawling the local council's website about the disposal of roadkill. 'I rang Dylan, and he said you'd just left.' I nod. 'I'm sorry. Your father, and now this. How do you feel?' he adds, looking not into my eyes but at my forehead, as if captivated by the activity in my brain. All I can think of are scenes in TV dramas when parents are told their child has died. I ought to feel grief-stricken. But I don't. I feel triumph. My rival is dead.

'Do you think she was in pain before, um, before she—?'

'It wasn't Tallulah, actually. It was Tim,' Matt interrupts, softly.

Tim. Timid Tim. Daring for once to be adventurous – to be something he wasn't. The pain in the back of my legs intensifies, making me gasp, and for a moment I hear a dreadful rushing noise in my ears. Hot tears drip down my cheeks. How could this have happened? And all the time the thoughts in my head are wild and jumbled up with fury, fury that the wrong one has died.

Chapter Fifteen

DYLAN INSISTS on conducting the funeral. I insist that the funeral be held after I've completed my new business pitch. The RSPCA in the meantime insists that the plastic bag containing Tim should be stored in the freezer. Which is why, on Monday night, Matt and I are forced to eat the defrosted home-made stew from the bottom drawer, even though the bottom drawer of the freezer contains, according to my laminated schedule hanging in the utility room, food only for Fridays. I make a mental note to buy another freezer.

*

I sit in the lobby of the headquarters of Keswick Ramsay plc. The building's granite-clad exterior suggests commendable Scottish thrift. Inside, a triple-height atrium of chrome and dusky-pink marble hints at opulence and success. The subliminal message is of shrewd money-management.

Since my arrival twenty minutes ago, I have twice visited the bathroom. Now, in the lobby, sweat dribbles down the side of my waist under my blouse.

Suppressing my fury at Tim's demise, or rather his sister's suspicious survival, I am trying to be conscientious. The combination of my pitch, my track record in the industry and my reputation for persuading candidates to work for unattractive companies gives me a strong chance. I have an instinct for detail. Attending to details makes me feel safe.

So my nerves aren't due to the imminent meeting. Rather, they are linked to a note I wrote my mother – as yet unsent, and currently polluting my briefcase, pending amendments or being torn up.

While Matt was placing the dearly departed in 'Vegetables: Friday', I was seized by a surge of venom, which no amount of logical thought would exhaust. The dozy boy, who rarely strayed further than his food bowl, had been crushed; the girl had lived. Something in the world had gone awry, and I found my rage displaced into rabid prose. I scribbled in the way one's mind scrolls back through time, thoughts spinning off at tangents, so that soon the original starting point is forgotten. Matt, who approves of (no, *champions*!) emotional honesty, appeared once with a mug of strong black coffee, and massaged my shoulders, and then retired to bed to watch the golf highlights. Eventually, I stopped writing and read the pages back through. The words were lacerating, but they made no sense at all. They didn't explain why today, as an adult, I feel so angry, so ruptured from within that I fear I will explode.

I didn't crawl into bed until three o'clock, by which time I'd not only completed Wednesday's business pitch, but also shredded the letter. Then I'd seized a postcard, and in one sentence informed my mother that we need to speak.

*

My name is being called. I stand up with purpose, and reach for my briefcase. Straightening, I come face to face with a man wearing the look of a train spotter on his first day at Clapham Junction.

'Fergus,' I say, with a weary smile. In a blink I take in the same pinstriped trousers, the same square buckles on his shoes. Thankfully, today he is without the lethal beaker of coffee, but even so, to my shame, at his approach I take a step back.

He'd sent me, as I knew he would, his résumé. No qualification, however small, had gone unmentioned (his certificates are framed and displayed, somewhere, I am sure). He observes closely the conventions of formal British speech and dress; he holds the gaze of a person when speaking; he remembers people's names. My fantasy is that he spends so much time reading self-help books on how to get ahead in business that he leaves himself no time to make any progress.

'So, Amber. May I ask, what are you doing here?'

Without waiting for my reply, he leans in and whispers that he's been 'doing the needful'. I take this to mean that he's been having lots of meetings that he would imagine are interviews, but which are really chats with bored human resources staff.

As he stands upright once more, he steps back on to the foot of the receptionist from the directors' floor, who has come to tell me that my meeting is further delayed. After apologies from both parties, Fergus asks me whether I'd care for an early lunch (*I'll try not to spill my coffee this time*). As he speaks, he hops, jack-knifing one thigh on which to balance his briefcase, searching for his coffee-shop loyalty card. I'm about to decline his offer when I catch a glimpse inside his briefcase. It is empty, containing nothing more than a few biros and a battered copy of *Mr Phillips*. I look up into his eyes – they are as wide and round as a seal pup's, liquid brown and innocent.

*

Later that afternoon, inside Ginny's flat, I wriggle my toes in the soapy water. I am trying to breathe deeply (in through the nose, out through the mouth), to banish a tightness in my chest. The coffee I had with Fergus made with real milk surely accounts for my discomfort. I enjoyed my time with Fergus. He has not yet informed his parents, whose son is 'something oversized in London', that he's currently unemployed. So we are both hiding!

The presentation went well. The board like my suggestion of the one candidate whose Washington contacts would give the bank unfettered access to decision-makers in Congress. I can expect to hear by the end of the week.

Which leaves the unposted postcard. I feel faintly nauseous.

'Why', Ginny asks, 'can't you just phone your mother?'

'Because,' I begin, limply, then hesitate. What I want to describe is too subtle, too hard to pin down; how all my previous calls to my mother miraculously coincide with a visitor at her door (*I can't talk to you now*). Telephoning is out of the question. I'm not prepared to suffer the humiliation of being so easily rebuffed.

Out in the street, the autumn evening air is unexpectedly icy. I hail a cab, and think again of Fergus. Inept, kind-hearted Fergus. The man defined by his chewed-up pens. His reluctance to tell his parents the truth might be amusing. It might encapsulate his shortcomings, those of a man unaware that his coffee had left a thick moustache of foam on his upper lip – indeed who chose his drink precisely because he thought '*macchiato*' is pronounced like 'macho'. But even as I want to laugh *at* him, in some sense I've started to wonder whether he and I aren't frighteningly alike, especially in the way we've both worked hard to escape, to erect barriers to withstand parental assault by accusation. In short, to turn ourselves into other people.

I switch on the intercom and tell the driver what I'm looking for. Before long, he has pulled up at the kerb. I get out, leaving my laptop on the seat. Then I reach into my briefcase, retrieve the postcard and bring it up to the slot in the wall. I scan the list of collecting times. Behind me, a horn toots. Looking back, I see a red postal van urging my taxi to move along, eager to perform the seven o'clock collection.

I reread the sentence on the card one final time, and then drop it through the slot.

Chapter Sixteen

THE TELEPHONE CALL comes on Friday morning. Afterwards, I send Nicole a text.

I buy U thin caf. NOW
2 busy
+ blueberry muffin?
Done

Later, we order more coffees, two more cakes, before returning to our stools in the coffee-shop window. (*We regret to inform you of the permanent closure as of today of the staff canteen. We wish to thank you for your custom and support over the years.*)

'When will you go, yaar?' asks Nicole, twisting a rope of chocolate hair around her finger, and eyeing my latest muffin.

'Early next week.'

'That soon! Aren't you nervous?'

'Terrified!' I push my cake towards Nicole. 'A bit sick, actually. I need to write down everything I'm going to say.'

'Thanks. I've got a real sugar craving at the moment. Nearly time of the month. Typical.'

I tell her how I plan to bake lots of sweet things for Tim's funeral tomorrow – for the children, of course.

'Why bother?' says Nicole, her mouth full of refined inverted sugars. 'Just buy it in.' She swallows. 'You always cook far too much food, anyway.'

I feel as though I've just been slapped – although Nicole does have a point. Why do I always go to so much trouble? Dylan's hailing it a celebration of a life, when actually it's a sodding party for a crushed *cat*.

Nicole polishes off my muffin. I can still recall the shock of watching her unpack pots of home-made chutney and green tins of Milo from her trunk in college. At the time, I was embarrassed for her, wondering what kind of mother imagines that food cannot be purchased away from home.

'So,' says Nicole, screwing up the paper case and dropping it into her coffee cup. 'What are you going to say?'

'I'm hoping to say very little, to see what gets revealed.'

'So why have you got me here, apart from to gloat?'

'I need your advice,' I say, producing a plastic folder containing draft questions.

Nicole extracts her laptop from her grosgrain bag, and plugs it into a small socket at the far end of the counter. Then she tucks her chocolate column behind her ears and calls up a clean document. And over the next half an hour, united by a love of the well-timed, penetrating question to dismantle even the most defended personality, we construct a proposal containing just the right amount of flattery, deference and interrogation, finishing with expressions of warmth to seal a commitment. Certain relationships, we know, demand meticulous manipulation. Keswick's will be proud.

'Now it's my turn for some T-L-C,' says Nicole in a fake American drawl, as she slides the laptop between its grosgrain covers. 'Do you think that if Dominic and I split up, I'd be sad? I mean, I know I'd be sad, but I'm sure I'd cope. Do you think I'd cope?'

I tap the pages of my questions on the counter top to line them up. 'Are you about to?'

'Absolutely not.'

'So what's the problem?'

'Well, I've been quite jittery lately. I thought maybe I was getting bored with him.'

'Bored?'

'Well, not bored exactly. But since Rex introduced the quarterly performance tables, we've been working so hard, the only time Dominic and I spend together is at the morning meetings.'

I look at her. Her beautiful skin appears for once to have lost its luscious bloom. Or perhaps it's the lighting in this coffee shop. 'Remember – quality not quantity.'

'In which case, I *know* I'm bored! All relationships mutate over time.'

Out in the street, we rub cheekbones and go our separate ways: Nicole, to Boots for some aspirin; and me to my desk, to keep vigil.

As the afternoon wears on, a headache creeps down my neck and fans out across my shoulders. I assume I'm starting a cold. I think of borrowing some of Nicole's aspirin. But I resist, trusting in the need to remain alert.

Because Nicole is wrong. Her theory is mere speculation. Not all relationships change. Some are wounds that weep without end.

Which just leaves the other telephone call. The one I've been dreading. Which never comes.

Chapter Seventeen

IN THE END, Jenny sings an extract from Fauré's Requiem, in such a neck-prickling way as to make you feel she understands intimately something of the sorrow in the music; Eloise reads (I trust I won't be thought biased here) a wonderful poem she wrote herself, rhyming 'Tim' with 'Heavin'; Dylan delivers the liturgy with a catch in his voice; and David plies him with tissues for his allergy to cat fur. Privately I doubt that *frozen* cat fur has any potency, and detect more than a whiff of melodrama. Finally, just as the ache in everyone's lower back reaches unbearable proportions, the crowd (which includes amused onlookers such as Nicole, who thinks all cats are mangy and has really only come to catch up with friends) take turns to sprinkle soil over the corpse. Then it's inside for cake, and bread and butter.

Tallulah, I notice, has been conspicuously absent for some days. Perhaps she knows that I've been scanning eBay for a section on selling female cats. Look, I want to say (to anyone who'll listen): *she's fickle. She's the embodiment of conditional love. To engage with this creature would destroy me.* But I know to keep such daft thoughts to myself.

I hear Dylan in the room above start playing the piano, so I grab a plate of shop-bought (hey!) fondant fancies and go upstairs. He sits hunched over the keyboard, his unruly ginger curls bobbing metronomically. Emily and Eloise sit on the piano stool beside him and are enthralled, as though he's a saint and they've been hypnotised by his halo.

117

Suddenly I notice that Matt is sitting on the sofa, a beer in one hand, his legs slightly apart, the beer can resting on one thigh. And Tallulah in his lap, nestling in the sacred triangle where I thought only I was allowed to go. Notwithstanding the question as to how she has slipped under my highly vigilant radar, what the fuck is she doing with my husband? He is a vision of contentment, a slight smile on his face, listening to the music and scratching the cat under her chin. Most cats would be sitting with their eyes half-closed, lost in the pleasure of the moment. Tallulah's are wide open, staring directly at me. They spear me with a long lance of jousts won.

'Aunty Amber's dropped all the cakes on the floor,' gurgle Emily and Eloise, sliding off the stool with such speed you'd have thought they'd been praying for something like this to happen all day. They pounce for the food at my feet, caring not that my shins are in the way. In my hand, at my side, rests an empty plate.

No one else reacts to what has just happened; to the way the world has just flipped inside out. Dylan carries on playing, and sneaks a quick drag of something hand-made. The girls have gathered up the cakes in the skirts of their dresses and are transporting the booty to under the piano. Matt takes a sip of beer, apparently mesmerised by scratching the cat. Only one pair of eyes remains trained on me, dominating the space between us. On my way down to the basement I have to stop where the stairs twist back on themselves to lean my head against the cool wall. Is this what it feels like to start losing your mind?

Once down in the kitchen, I find the women rinsing cutlery, and chatting. Serena looks up.

'That'll be the girls,' she says, smiling at the sudden discordant sounds beyond the ceiling, of keys being randomly depressed. 'Sometimes I think they're boys in disguise.'

'They're just being loud and annoying, as usual,' announces Eleanor, Serena and Harry's eldest by eleven months. I decide not to reveal how her sisters have overdosed on sugar.

'Eleanor,' I say quickly, 'I'm putting you in charge of—', I stop myself just in time from saying 'torturing Tallulah', '—of finding out who wants tea and who wants coffee.'

I want Eleanor to know that I trust her with responsibility. But now, watching her skip upstairs, I sense I've inadvertently re-inforced a narrow range of options open to women. Why didn't I say: *Eleanor, I'm putting you in charge of finding the cure for cancer*; or *finding out whether the SLK is better than the Z3*; or *why mothers don't always love their children*—?

Enough, I snap to myself, and begin to lay out fresh cakes. Upstairs I can hear that Dylan's begun to play some Sondheim. Which is lucky, as Sondheim always puts me in a good mood.

Dylan and I worship at the shrine of Stephen Sondheim. I revere him for his verbal dexterity and innovative autopsies on modern relationships; Dylan translates this to mean that, lyrically, Sondheim's a bloody genius: 'Someone to hold you too close, Someone to hurt you too deep, Someone to sit in your chair, To ruin your sleep'.

Matt has never quite seen the attraction, despite forced atten-dance at many productions. You, he will often tease Dylan, are the author of a (rejected) song for the school rock band, 'Inaugural Suicide', a ditty which began, 'Why did she flee the party? Why did she steal the Maserati?' Dylan, Matt will add, is therefore perhaps underqualified to comment on lyrical brilliance. Of course, Dylan and I concede, certain Sondheim works are flawed – the original Broadway run of *Anyone Can Whistle* only lasted a week. But our adoration is hard to dismantle. It smacks, Matt warns with a certain superiority, of children idolising their parents.

I like to think my adoration is the more authentic. That it isn't as slavish as Dylan's, as illustrated by my capacity to actually *dislike* some of the canon. *Assassins*, for example, which I find bitty. Naturally, we have our favourites: Dylan, appropriately, cries over 'Giants in the Sky', from *Into the Woods*; I like 'Old Friends', from *Merrily We Roll Along*. But our favourite musical is *Company*.

Dylan turns round, suspending the bridge of 'What Would We Do Without You?' His hands linger on the keyboard. He sees my eyes glistening with tears, and gives a small nod. Then he turns back and continues playing. Clearly he thinks I'm engaged with the music.

Instead, I'm staring at the photos propped up on the piano: our wedding, Eloise at the twins' christening, Dylan's ordination. Matt waterskiing, our honeymoon on safari, eating noodles in Cambodia. Serena with one-hour-old twins, Jenny in a large hat, me in a veil, me and Dylan in mortar boards. Me smiling.

By nightfall, everyone is upstairs, singing round the piano – even Matt, despite the fact that he hasn't performed publicly since *HMS Pinafore* at prep school; in a dress. Eleanor turns the pages, while her sisters whirl to the music, pretending to be sycamore keys in the wind, their pale hair floating behind them, before falling asleep on the sofa.

'Auditions are on Tuesday,' Dylan reminds us all, to a chorus of groans. I retreat downstairs to put together a tray of cheese and biscuits. Harry is teasing Dylan that he's snaffled the lead part for himself.

'I need to talk to you, yaar.' Nicole has followed me down, in pedicured barefoot silence.

'So you *are* dumping Dominic.'

'Nooo,' says Nicole slowly. 'At least, I haven't thought everything through yet.'

'What "everything"?' I say, tapping a digestive as I pick it up, to shed loose crumbs.

Nicole finds my wrist and grips it. 'I'm pregnant.'

Chapter Eighteen

I SPEED UP on the road south out of London; the car might as well be fuelled with delirium. I check my rear-view mirror constantly.

Every so often, I realise that I'm holding my breath. My mind flounders in its own birthing pool, bobbing in the water to avoid the word – my greatest fear. A word with angry blue veins across its taut, hard belly. Pregnant. So Nicole is pregnant. The expensive toy whose body now contains Fabergé fertilised eggs. First two cells, then four, then however many. Billions of cells, endlessly, endlessly multiplying. Unless. Unless?

Last night, that other word got stuck in my throat. But apparently there is to be no disposal, no end to this chain of reproduction. Indeed the opposite would appear to hold sway, since Nicole now speaks as though her world has turned pink and glittery overnight. This was my cue to enthuse, to congratulate. *But I'm sorry*, Nicole kept saying. She assumed I disapproved. And it's true: I've turned into my mother. I've inherited her disapproval, like haemophilia.

I press my foot down further on the accelerator.

As distances to Mother's village begin appearing on road signs, I know I've made a dreadful mistake. It's not in my nature to be reckless, and rushing after a sleepless night to face her without proper planning is as reckless an act as I can envisage. As reckless as coming off the pill. I spot signs for Midhurst, and swerve across three lanes.

Midhurst is one large teashop. I enter one, with its smell of mothballs. Little nonagenarians, shrunken with osteoporosis and wearing their hats indoors, stare at me as I sit down. My tea comes quickly; the toasted teacakes glisten with forbidden butter. Maybe my anxiety has been triggered by nothing more pathological than an empty stomach.

Soon, the tearoom is packed with mothers piloting pushchairs. A beautiful redhead asks to borrow a chair from my table. Her breasts are enormous, their skin creamy yet freckled, squeezed into a little green top whose scoop-neck trumpets rather than hides their ripeness. I am ensnared by the banter of these women, their confidence, their sensuality, even though they all have their backs to me. Lucky Nicole. I am the child skipping on her own in the playground, while all the others play 'All In Together Girls'.

And I try to imagine what it might be like to find out that one is already three months pregnant. To have the decision largely taken out of one's hands. As if that could ever happen! And yet this Masonic Lodge of the Tearoom is fiercely debating that very thing; a local teenager who gave birth in the school toilets, apparently unaware she was pregnant.

Nicole, it seems, has always known. In the beginning, she tried to deny what, with her sudden cravings for my muffins and attacks of giddiness in the London Eye, she'd suspected all along. But it was only at the twins' birthday party, when just the smell of wine had made her want to retch, that she decided to pay attention. And even then it had taken her a couple of weeks to pluck up the courage to go to Boots and buy the testing kit.

As I pull the door to the teashop behind me, my face feels slapped by the brisk autumn wind in the high street. Slowly I walk to my car. Matt will be on the golf course by now, his mobile switched off. I hoped this morning that he'd cancel his game, to be by my side, but he didn't. We had a row, or rather I chucked a few toys out of my pram while Matt checked the contents of his golf bag. I've been married to a psych for long enough to know that boundaries are not made to be broken, especially sporting ones. I hate the way he does what he does for a living and yet can't magic my heartache away.

*

A sea breeze tacks across the salt marshes and stings my cheeks. I squeeze my hands into the pockets of my jeans, and wish I'd brought a jumper. I'd forgotten how much the temperature drops away from London. Looking up, I catch sight in the distance of Mother's maroon bungalow, a converted Victorian railway carriage. I stumble on some loose earth on the footpath.

I reach the place where the path forks. It peels away to the left towards the mudflats and shingle beds of the southern spit; the start of the internationally famous, protected-status ornithological trail. I hesitate. Is something moving over by the carriage? Someone stepping outside to empty tea leaves? Someone hurrying back inside? But with the grass swaying in the breeze, the glare of the sun on the wetlands (the tide is coming in) and the cries of birds, I can't be sure. Ignoring the weather-worn sign forbidding entry which Mother fought lengthy battles with the council to erect (*for my privacy*) (*So don't live alongside a tourist attraction, Mother*), I walk towards the carriage. My heart is knocking against my ribcage.

The bungalow appears to be empty. Its windows are closed. Dead plants in a window box stutter in the wind. Weeds surround the brackets that secure the carriage to its foundations. The carriages were brought to the village after the First World War to combat a housing shortage, positioned in the woodlands just beyond the reserve boundary. In May 1944, fifty 6,000-ton sections of the Mulberry Harbour to be used in Operation Overlord were secretly stored here prior to the invasion. The carriage Mother now owns was moved closer to the lagoon mouth to house the small unit of soldiers guarding these temporary naval migrants. Which is also why its nearest neighbour stands such a distance away in the copse.

When others of her generation are moving closer to grandchildren, or contemplating sheltered accommodation, my mother selects somewhere remote. She has a history of anaemia. Sickle cell traits have been mooted. I've lost track of the number of times childhood treats, trips to the zoo or the cinema, were held hostage to Mother's attacks of palpitations. And it's my fear that one night I'll receive a call from the police who, having been alerted by twitchers, have broken down the carriage door to discover a decomposing body – mother's final triumph, an everlasting accusation of neglect from someone who keeps the world at bay.

As I approach the carriage from the path, gulls screech their siren warnings. I knock and wait for the door to be opened. White clouds scud in front of the sun, and I shiver. Do I want my mother to be home, or not? It occurs to me that she might be on holiday, although holidays are for people with an appetite for pleasure. Perhaps she's out enjoying the hospitality of the many friends whose arrival so often coincides with my phone calls. I knock again, and cup my hands around my ears to blot out the sound of the wind and the birds.

After a few minutes, I circle the carriage, placing each footstep on the shingle so as to make as little noise as possible. I'm hoping to catch my mother out, to glimpse her through a window, hiding in some fashion, and to expose her in some way. But I see nothing meriting reproach, and as the wind tosses my hair across my face, I feel foolish and dishevelled.

I walk back to the fork and, on a whim, take the path towards the visitors' centre. From here, I slide gingerly down the grass bank to the hide from where years ago my school class would watch birds feeding on the mudflats.

Inside, I find a family of twitchers dressed in blue cagoules. They are watching, they whisper, three rare curlew sandpipers. The son, who looks to be about ten or eleven, is making careful notes in a pocketbook. Father is in charge of the binoculars. He passes them to me, and shows me where to look. I see them immediately, the russet flush on their bellies, their eyes rimmed with white. Along the flood embankment I can make out the old school building, now derelict. The mother passes me some black coffee. We all sit, our silence punctuated by the distant cries of birds. My ears still burn from the cold, and my nose runs from the coffee steam, but it's good to be out of the wind. When I've finished, I hand back the cup before creeping out of the hide, my final smile thanking them for their easy company.

As I approach the car, I see the parking ticket tucked under the wiper. I scan the hedgerows for a notice. So, provincial wardens are as officious as their urban cousins. Matt will certainly see the funny side. But as I reach out for the ticket I recognise mother's tiny hand-writing. My heart thumping, I read the message, its edges frayed where Mother (an evacuee, hard-wired to economise) has folded and torn some random mailshot into four, to use as scrap.

I bang on the carriage door repeatedly. 'I know you're in there'. The wind snatches my words away. It occurs to me that Mother is not in the carriage at all, but is watching from the copse behind. I turn, fully expecting to see her sitting on a fence, gloating. But all I see is a vast expanse of windswept wasteland leading to a Brothers Grimm woodland. I shout through the letterbox. The pull-down window of the carriage door was replaced with a wooden panel for security reasons when the carriages were first erected. In despair, and in some sense still convinced that Mother is not at home, I start swearing.

'I should make you come inside and wash your mouth out with soap.'

My spine locks. The voice seems to belong to the wind. And yet it's unmistakably Mother's timbre, uttering chillingly familiar senti-ments. I push open the letterbox.

'Mother?' I pause, straining to hear sounds inside. 'Where are you?'

'That sounds more civilised.' The voice comes from just beyond the door – in the shadows.

'Why won't you open the door?'

'And have to listen to you screaming at me in my small home?'

'But I'm only screaming out here because – oh, for goodness sake.' I sink my chin towards my chest and try to calm down, to not rise to the bait. I must not ask again to be let in. It would hand Mother an easy victory.

'This note you left on my car. What does it mean?'

'It means what it says. What was it you studied at university? English? Dear me, does Matt do all your reading for you now, as well? And I did try *so* hard to make it simple.'

How quickly it always comes to this, I think. *This bitterness, from a woman who never finished school.*

'It's certainly very concise.'

'Well, there's no point in wasting good ink.'

The cloud cover thickens and steals away the sun.

'Anyway, thank you for coming,' I hear her say, as if to trade.

'Aren't you even interested in finding out why I'm here?'

'I told you in my note. I got your postcard. Now, I have a very busy afternoon—'

'Do you really think I'd drive all this way just to find out whether you got it?'

'Why else would you be here? It couldn't possibly be to spend time with your poor old Mum. You never were a daughter who visits, or brought friends to eat round my table.'

'You never cook!'

'I gave up when you refused my cheese tart.'

'I can't eat dairy. You know that.'

'What kind of child refuses milk?'

I shut my eyes at the familiarity, the futility, of this particular dispute. A crow hops on the pebbles around me, emitting its Dalek war cry.

'My card told you we needed to talk. I'm here to talk to you.'

'And we have spoken. Now, I need to get on.'

I shiver on the shingle. It's as though Mother has stolen all the warmth in the world; not because she wants it particularly, but to prevent others from having the pleasure.

I'm about to go, when for no reason at all I recall Serena telling me at Tim's funeral that Esme has become stroppy at mealtimes, hurling her bowl on the floor and refusing to eat. Serena feigns disinterest, but she's concerned and annoyed. She reasons that she doesn't have time to indulge the child. Esme will eat what everyone else eats, and what doesn't get eaten will be left in the bowl until it is.

And so I shout, without pausing for breath, that Dad is dead; that there was a funeral and that Mother was banned. And then I sprint back to the fork in the path before she has a chance to hurl this information back in my face.

From the fork I run to the car without looking back, get inside and drive away. My legs are shaking so much it is impossible to use the clutch, and so I drive for several miles in first gear, the engine roaring with the effort. I feel, not that I am lost, but that I am numb, my emotions swallowed by the orange orb of the sun I see in my rear-view mirror, as it slinks behind the glorious swell of the Downs. Only once I cross the county border some thirty miles away do I pull over and weep hot tears.

Chapter Nineteen

THE NEXT DAY I fly into New York where, in an air-conditioned room at a discreet SoHo hotel, I've arranged to interview my candidate for Keswick's. It's a meeting arranged on the tacit understanding that neither side will reveal our connection. Former patients are often flattered to be rung up by their erstwhile psychiatrist. Particularly if there's a favour involved. Especially those recalling a crisis of great personal, if not national, disquiet. Even more so if issues of secrecy had been so vital that the psychiatrist had been sourced from abroad, with consultations conducted on the golf course to foil an intrusive international media.

And so this former patient has agreed to meet his psychiatrist's wife. I suspect my call could not have been better timed. People don't give much thought to the fact that, after you've held powerful office, you might be stuck, on a long-term basis, for something to actually do. But I do give such things due thought. In psychological terms, I know just which levers to pull. I know that successful people do not succeed by chance. They are all driven to avenge an early hurt, and this drive never dies. It becomes their vocation. I know this viscerally, because it underpins my very soul. And knowledge, they say, is power. When I meet successful people, I see the wounded child inside.

Rage at my mother's rejection has dulled my excitement at the task ahead. Throughout the flight, I am listless and weepy in turns; I keep having to disappear to the toilet to replenish tissue supplies.

The rest of the time, I burrow into my cradle chair, ignoring the food and entertainment. It isn't until I cross the threshold of the hotel room that I imagine the mask of the functioning adult snap back into place. I watch as two bodyguards step outside to take up positions in the corridor. They smile as they register my tailored skirt and expensive heels.

My candidate pours me coffee. From the writing desk he picks up a copy of my book, *The Right Job for You*, and asks me to sign it. In spite (or perhaps as a result) of having a face resembling an excited marsupial, this is a man with a well-polished instinct for intimacy. He combines charm with intelligence. Every look, every word, vibrates with significance. Above all, I sense in him the hunger of someone damaged early in life perpetually striving to amend the deficits.

He massages away any doubts I might have regarding his suitability for the role. He proves himself extremely well briefed: about Keswick's, naturally, but also about me. He makes me feel that of all the people he's ever met, I am by far the most fascinating. He knows the subject of my university dissertation (*I just adore Edith Wharton*), and how much my bonus was last year (*that's impressive, Amber!*). There's even soya milk in a jug with the coffee (*I'm lactose-intolerant, too – doesn't it suck?*). In his openness, and abundant emotional curiosity, I am reminded of Matt.

Once I leave the hotel and the aura of the man's charisma, I feel bereft.

The heat in the city is as oppressive as in London. Sensible folk will be staying away until after Labour Day. For a while I wander aimlessly. I drift around boutiques, fingering impossibly wispy pieces of fabric. A vague plan to buy designer foodstuffs at Dean & DeLuca is thwarted when I find it closed for the day to be used as a film set.

Eventually I find myself at Ground Zero. I clink in my heels up a metal staircase and stand on the raised iron platform. I stare into the crater below. My feet have swollen in the heat. They are sore where the tight leather chafes my skin. Leaning into a railing, I ease one blistered foot out of its shoe.

Nothing has prepared me for this scene of desolation, the way the vast expanse of concrete flooring shimmers in the heat and appears to stretch to the horizon. The clang of metal on metal drifts upwards. Traffic hums in the background. The sun shines fiercely, bright and defiant. Workmen go about their business, wearing hard hats, their bronzed torsos stripped to the waist. And, in the face of their physicality, their task of active regeneration, I suddenly feel hollow, diminished. It is as though the question with my mother has always been: which headhunter will claim the first scalp? And I am suddenly hijacked by the desire to step off the ledge and never be bothered by her again.

*

The return flight that night is empty. Despite the flat beds, and the entertainment options, I am restless. My mother lurks in the background like a particularly bothersome flight attendant.

I am one of only a handful of passengers on my deck. All are sleeping, having eaten in the Club lounge prior to boarding. The crew, taking advantage of the slack, gossip in secret recesses beyond the galley. I assume I am the only one awake. I ease myself up in the darkness and prise off my eye mask. The beds are arranged nose to tail, as though in homage to some unspoken erotic pleasure. To my astonishment I lock eyes with my neighbour, who has paused in his reading of the latest John Updike. He peers over the top of his spectacles.

'Jet lag?' he mouths.

I grin and shake my head. 'Pathetic, isn't it!' I whisper. 'It's three in the morning our time, and I'm wide awake!'

'I know the feeling.' The man removes his reading glasses. Late forties, I reckon. A youthful fifty at most. Clean-shaven, despite the hour, and with groomed greying hair. He wears a white linen shirt, which hangs in soft folds around his chest. Attractive laughter lines draw attention to his eyes, which are the luscious colour of washed mangoes. His accent is appropriately mid-Atlantic. 'So, what were you in town for? Business or pleasure?'

Believing it would be disingenuous to imply hard graft when the meeting had proved so exhilarating (*Now, whaddya say we order in lunch, Amber!*), I admit to a bit of both. The stranger rolls his eyes as if to say, *Isn't that so New York?*

We've reached that awkward border crossing when conversing with strangers, a checkpoint between intimacy and solitude. To snuggle back into my cubicle might be misconstrued as a snub, yet to prolong conversation with a man who'd made arrangements to consort with literary nobility seems laced with presumption.

And then it comes to me, unbidden as it were. That we float here in limbo, thousands of feet above the clouds, suspended between time zones. We can somersault beyond the gravitational pull of real life, into spaces beyond the reach of criticism, to experience free will in its purest form, unfettered by assumptions, mistakes or consequences; language, religion or nation. No background, no baggage. To meet without prejudice. To have not even traded names. To know only this: that to be human is to be free.

I unbuckle my seatbelt, toss my blanket to the floor and step round to his cubicle. With his leg, he kicks the footrest into upright and leans forward to secure it; there is no pretence between us that

I've merely come to chat. I hold his gaze before moving to stand before him, sliding my skirt and silk lining up over my thighs. He grasps my buttocks with large warm hands and pulls me gently towards him. I notice the smooth triangle of toffee skin at his neck where the top button is undone. I place a fingertip in the groove and stroke it lightly. His scent is subtle: an intoxicating blend of clean skin, musk and warm intelligence. I straddle him, and as he unzips himself I sink my knees into his seat. He kisses me forcefully, missing my mouth and almost biting my cheek, twisting my head to align our lips. His hand finds my knickers. He parts them slightly, and slides his finger inside me. My knees are sore from the seat's rough fabric, but it does give very good leverage. Slowly I lower myself on to him.

From the floor, John Updike's dust jacket smile observes us, as if in approbation.

*

In a shower cubicle in the airport Club lounge, I press my forehead into the cold tiles and close my eyes. Needles of water pierce my naked back. My head throbs. If only this was just due to dehydration. I grip both taps until my knuckles tinge white. Survival, I have always felt, is about staying in control. Right now, I don't recognise myself. I don't know this other person, this woman who's had sex with a stranger in the no-man's land above the clouds. I must regain control, if only to defy my mother's indifference. I have to retain control.

Chapter Twenty

B Y THE TIME I'm through passport control and have switched on my phone, I have four missed calls. Louisa has gone into premature labour. The messages, a typically easy-going one from Matt and three feral ones from the mother-to-be, overlap in the wish that I join them at the hospital. Prue is driving in from Norfolk. I try to focus in my taxi on the domestic drama unfolding in town, to obliterate memories of the subsonic one.

Which isn't easy. When I recall my duplicity, I feel utterly numb. Shame makes me fractious and I barrack the driver. And all around me the drabness of the suburbs and the chaos of endless roadworks match what I see as my festering inner ugliness. I rest my head against the window, as if the weight of guilt makes my skull too heavy for my neck.

William Edward, weighing in at less than four pounds, is sucked from Louisa's stomach as my cab draws up outside the hospital entrance. As I pay the fare, he is uttering his first whimper. As I spin the revolving doors and approach reception, his puce, wrinkled body is being sponged and rushed from theatre to incubator, to be wired up to monitors. And as I run down squeaky corridors, a sedated Louisa is being wheeled back to her room, and Matt is removing his sky-blue theatre scrubs and joking with the obstetrics team. When I arrive at the labour ward, I find beautiful, clean Matt sitting reading a dog-eared society magazine. I hug him so tightly he begins to laugh.

As we walk hand in hand to the vending machine, he describes the emergency Caesarean: how Louisa suffered potentially fatal side-effects to the drugs the hospital had administered to halt her contractions. Once these had been stopped, there was nothing the staff could do to delay William's arrival, and she'd been rushed to theatre. At one point, it was feared the baby might arrive in the lift, and the midwife had had to hold a pad in place to stop the low-lying placenta slipping out.

'I told Prue we'd wait till she got here,' whispers Matt, blowing on scalding liquid once we reach Louisa's room. 'Is that all right? You look bushed. Couldn't you sleep on the plane?'

Sometimes when Matt is tired, his voice has a stronger Springbok lilt. It reminds me that he was once a little boy in another country far away, and I long to wrap him up in a blanket. I close my eyes. Against his shoulder, I am Sleeping Beauty. I listen as Matt speaks, with his easy grasp of medical terminology, hacking at the briars of blood, and mucus, and morphine, before saving me with a kiss.

Sometimes I fantasise that I am one of his patients; that he will sit on my bed and make all my horrid feelings go away. And sometimes when I'm in a really self-pitying mood, I will tell him this; and Matt will laugh and say I could never afford his fees.

Louisa utters a moan just as Prue appears in the doorway – as though, even in sleep, she can sense her mother's approach. As if the very air around a mother quivers with the static of maternal concern. Matt and I stand up.

'How is she?' gasps Prue, to no one in particular. Her voice is taut, her words clipped.

At the sight of her mother, Louisa begins to weep. 'They put a needle in my hand', she mumbles repeatedly, and 'Why weren't you here?' Prue sits on the bed and strokes Louisa's fringe, ignoring the reproaches. She murmurs soothing sounds. Then she leans forward and gently kisses the new mother's forehead.

I suddenly feel very clammy. I offer to fetch Prue a coffee.

As the liquid spurts into the cup, tears stream down my face and splash on to my shoes.

Chapter Twenty-one

OF ALL THE FRIENDS whose telephones throb with news of William's premature arrival, one in particular has specific reason to thank He who moves in mysterious ways – for the birth proves to be indirectly responsible for the unusually high attendance at Dylan's auditions. That evening, as we cram around Louisa's bed, the gang finds itself unwittingly in Dylan's parish. And, when Louisa becomes too weary for visitors, there is clearly (even for those who traditionally hide their social inertia behind a lack of childcare) no escape, as Dylan cheerily reminds us.

Owing to a church hall timetable clash – a beetle drive for the local Youth Re-offending Team – we gather in the church itself. It feels different when not set up for a service. For one thing, all the heavy wooden pews have been moved to the sides, creating an empty space that appears to make our footsteps ring out more loudly on the flagstones. The triptych of stained-glass windows seems flatter, somehow, without bright sunlight pouring through them. And, without fresh flowers, or people in their Sunday best, I feel as though I'm trespassing on something intensely private.

Just one area looks the same. At either side of the shallow steps leading to the chancel stand the wooden pedestal of a carved statue of the Virgin Mary, painted cream and blue, and an iron lectern with the wings of a bronze eagle forming the bookrest. Behind them I can see the altar draped in white cloth, topped with two burning candles, their flames flickering in the reredos of beaten gold.

On the rare occasions I go to church, these objects barely register. But tonight, I feel glad to see them. *We're here for you*, they seem to say. *We'll always be here.*

On one of the pews sits a clique of strangers. They glare at me as I nod at them and smile. Their eyes appear dark and lifeless. Dylan sidles up to me.

'Don't waste your breath trying to make them like you,' he whispers. 'Their jealousy of each other is exceeded only by their hatred of new people.'

Dylan stands on the steps to the chancel and, adopting the single malt undertone he reserves for making parishioners do things they don't want to do, urges us to form a circle for some warm-up exercises. Beneath the scraping of shoes on flagstones, there are detectable ripples of discontent, which Dylan bravely ignores. How, I ask myself, does he remain so upbeat amid such debilitating parish dynamics? No wonder he's thinking of leaving the church.

We are in the middle of a t'ai chi manoeuvre (led by Dylan whose knowledge of the art, learned on one of his retreats, is at best partial) when the west door is thrust aside by a figure resembling a female wizard. Wearing a diaphanous purple robe and menacing oversized treble-clef earrings, this creature strides to where the nave usually is.

'Sorry I'm late, darling,' she says, throatily. She air-kisses Dylan several inches from his cheeks, as though to avoid an infection. 'I couldn't tear myself away from Earl Spencer.'

Harry, standing to my left, leans in towards me and discreetly raises his eyebrows. 'She means the Earl of Spencer pub in Wandsworth.' I have to stifle a snort.

'Ladies and gentlemen, allow me to introduce Bea, your director for the show.' Dylan smiles beatifically. 'And may I say how very lucky we are to have secured her services,' he continues, which makes me think of dry-cleaners and tyre replacement concerns. Over near the Lady Chapel, the top crescents of the spectacles on the face of Julian, the church organist, are just visible above the parapet of the upright piano.

I watch this woman. Already I envisage conflict. It isn't that Bea resembles my mother in anything other than age. The most obvious difference is that Bea drapes her stockiness in flamboyant clothes, whereas my mother's pipe-cleaner frame prefers ration-coupon grey. Or camel, when under pressure to be sociable (not that I can ever recall my parents receiving invitations). Bea also models a technique for applying make-up that appears to consist of tossing the contents of her cosmetics bag into the air and standing underneath. But then she is a thespian, a career Bea is now detailing, from her salad days in the 1970s hoofing it naked in *Hair* – which frankly I don't believe – to directing one-off pilots for television; shows with unfamiliar names and obviously ignominious fortunes. 'She'll be telling us next she knew Noël Coward,' says Harry in a stage whisper of which Bea would be proud. Her performance contrives to be amusingly self-deprecating (at which laughing is mandatory) and, for me, conceited. It doesn't bode well. Already I can sense the power lines being drawn up.

'Why', I ask Dylan, in a break, 'did you get someone like her involved?'

Apparently Bea runs drama classes at a school where Dylan's a governor. It's obvious to me that, not only has he fallen under her Boadicean spell, but that he hopes she might act as a bulwark between him and Pamela.

God, how much energy we adults spend in trying to keep our parents at bay.

He asks after the audition I've just had.

'It was fine,' I say, casually. 'Julian played some scales which loosened my voice up nicely. And then, as I hand him my music, Bea asks me who my singing teacher is, and of course I have to confess I don't have one, so she gives me this passing-wind look before asking me what song I'm going to sing, and then, can you believe it, when I tell her she says, "Oh, but that's a black song. I have real issues with white girls doing obviously black songs—"'

'She called it a black song?' whispers Dylan. 'Streuth, she's worse than my mother—'

'I mean, it's George fucking Gershwin! How can anyone have an issue with that? So, yes, thanks for asking, my audition went brilliantly.'

'Well, hopefully she'll have been just as snooty to the parish clique, and they'll drop out. Primadonnas, every one. You can't believe how difficult they were over my plans for last Christmas's inaugural *In Excelsis Deo* extravaganza. I'd ordered dry ice and everything. And anyway, I've told Bea that if she doesn't give you a decent part, I'm pulling the show!'

'You can't do that,' I laugh.

'Why not? It's my gaff. It's my hall. I can do what I bloody well like.'

'Still, I'm not sure I can fit all the rehearsing in. I've got this huge project—'

'You've got to. This show's going to be my swan song. I want to go out with a bang.'

I gasp, and hold his gaze. 'A swan song? I'm afraid I have real issues with humans doing swan songs—'

Dylan pretends to throttle me.

The session after the break is exhausting. During a dance-through of the show's opening number, Dylan tries to avoid bumping into the statue of the Virgin Mary and collides instead with Jenny's angora-clad breasts. They both retire, feigning injury. When Bea next calls a break, everyone else collapses on to pews, facing each other from opposite sides of the nave – an audience at a medieval jousting contest.

'Couldn't you raise money for your roof by having a raffle, like other vicars?' groans Clive, who came to drop Jenny off at the audition and got bounced by Dylan into contorting his angle-poise joints into unnatural positions for the good of the chorus. 'Seriously, the lost opportunity costs, not to mention the low indicators of delivering on budget—' And there was me thinking management consultants were boring. Jenny tells her husband to shush. 'Anyway, I think I've got cramp,' he concludes, rolling up a trouser leg to knead the flesh of his skinny calf. Sitting next to him, I can't help noticing that this exposed leg is utterly hairless. Almost shiny, as though waxed. It's so abnormally smooth I have to will myself not to reach out and touch it, not least because it jars with the hirsute image Clive puts about with his abundant moustache. How little we know the people we know.

'I'd be fine if it wasn't for Bea,' says Harry, swigging tap water from a bottle recycled so often that what remains of the label is now white. 'You've found a right taskmaster there.'

'She's terrifying,' says Serena, who is peeling an orange and handing around segments. 'She reminds me of my old primary school teacher, a ghastly woman who played electric guitar and wore scarlet lipstick. Once, she came to school wearing a mantilla complete with black veil. I was off my food for a week I was so terrified.'

'You have unhappy memories of childhood?' I say.

'Oh God, yes. Who doesn't?' Serena turns to face me, a mother being scrupulously attentive to her child. My friends aren't just my family; they've become my parents. 'It's all changed now, of course, with marvellous people like Harry involved.' Here Serena leans forward to pat her husband's knee, which startles him, since he's talking to Jenny about the latest educational psychology on multiple-birth siblings. 'But back then I hated it. I had asthma, and was always off sick. And because both my parents worked, I was cared for by a succession of neighbours. And because I missed lots of classes, I was called stupid and idle. I swear I've spent more time in a primary school since Eleanor was born, what with parents' evenings and concerts, than I ever did as a child!'

I hold my tongue. So, it's *school* Serena hated, not childhood. I can identify with her neglect and confusion. It's the bearing five children I don't understand.

'So, how are we all?' Bea towers over us. Her Amazonian clefs seem to be pointing at us. But before anyone can reply she has moved in a swirl of fabric to grasp Jenny by the shoulders. 'You, child, are a delight to watch. Such a voice! With whom did you train?'

Jenny stutters a response.

'But that's impossible. Then you're a real natural.' And, having bestowed on Jenny the grace notes of her approbation, she turns on her kitten heels and bellows for Julian.

'My word, Jenny,' winks Harry, 'you're in there!'

*

Once inside our car, I kiss Matt. He smells of kebab, that faintly scandalous aroma of a man off the leash, left to his own culinary devices in the absence of his wife. Rex rang this evening, apparently, but I'm not interested. I urge Matt to just drive. He slips the car effortlessly into gear. 'So, how was it? Has my wife won the starring role she deserves?'

'Just drive,' I repeat, my smile fading, my jaw tightening.

'What's up?' he asks, reaching out to squeeze my knee.

'I'm not sure,' I say, and I begin to explain why I was late for the audition. How, as the friends had all shuffled out of Louisa's room, I heard her voice whisper my name …

*

I turned round to find the poor girl beginning to cry again. I moved to the bedside table and plucked some tissues from a box.

'Have you heard from Eddie?' she asked in a small voice. I had to confess that I had not.

'He shouldn't have come,' Louisa said, urgently.

'Ed's been here?' I said. How on earth had he got past Panzer Prue?

Louisa grimaced. 'Not Ed – Will.' Then she seized my wrist in an unnerving show of strength. 'It's all my fault. Promise me, Amber, you won't tell anyone. Not even my mother.' Her large, green eyes were fierce and flinty. I could see no alternative but to agree. Louisa relaxed her grip.

'They put a needle in my hand— I was exhausted, but they said— I was panicking, everyone was panicking, and the doctors— the doctors said, "I'm sorry Louisa, we have to get this baby out now", and I didn't want him to come out— but it was too late—'

I sat on the bed, stroking the girl's forehead, just as I'd seen Prue doing. How pitifully pale she looked beneath the harsh fluorescent lights, wrapped in a thin nightie. And how large were the dark stains around her sockets.

'—and then they put a mask on my face, and I couldn't breathe, I couldn't see— and the doctors were shouting to get the others— and I thought I was going to die, I thought I was splitting in two, that I was going to die— and the morphine— and they said, "He's got to come out now", and I knew it was wrong – it *is* wrong, Amber, isn't it? But there was nothing I could do—'

I shifted on the bed. I hadn't a clue what to say. Maybe it was her drugs. 'Nothing's wrong, Lou. William's in the best place, and so are you. You did brilliantly today! Matt told me—'

'It's all my fault. Oh Amber, help me. It's all my fault,' she wailed, gripping my arm even more tightly than before.

'You've done nothing wrong,' I murmured. Inside I felt a complete fraud. Louisa was now retching with sobs. I thought about alerting a member of staff.

'I kept saying no, but no one would listen— they drugged me and there was nothing I could do— he should never have come out. I wish he'd died, it's better that he dies. Please don't tell anyone I said that, but it is. And it's all my fault, I should never have kept this baby. I thought it would make Eddie come back— that he would want to see his own child—'

I felt a tremor ripple down my spine. It took me a moment to absorb this information. As I did so, my eyes rested on the forest of pastel cards propped on the cabinet. On the surface, the implication of Louisa's confession was preposterous. Surely women today didn't think that babies cement relationships? And yet here lay someone, of moderate intelligence one had thought, who had clearly assumed that they did.

'And now I know Ed won't ever come back— What can I do, Amber? Tell me what to do.' Louisa must have seen the confusion on my face, for she continued, 'I've always wanted to be like you—'

Louisa's monologue had the whiff of what girls at school called a 'pash'. 'To be honest, you're the only one of Eddie's friends I ever liked. Or, rather, you're the only one I thought liked me. I'm so much younger than all of you, and I was so desperate to be taken seriously. So when I realised I was expecting, I thought it would make me look grown-up.' Louisa gulped for air. 'I think that's why Ed stopped me seeing you all once my pregnancy was confirmed. I hoped it was because he was concerned, didn't want me overtired. But now I see it's because he hates the way I'm now linked to him for ever.

'I am so envious of you, Amber. You're so lucky, and free. Your life is your own, you can do whatever you want. Me, I've just repeated my mother's mistakes.'

At this, Louisa sank back into her pillow. I sat staring at my knees. Outside in the corridor, something large and metallic clattered to the floor; two members of staff roared with laughter. I felt waves of guilt at finding Louisa's distress so reassuring. So it was true: not everyone wanted babies. Not even once they'd had them. And, even if Louisa's gloom was short-lived and could be attributed to medication, or to the recent trauma of childbirth, or even to postnatal depression, which can be cured (*see* The Mother as Child: Psychiatric Treatment Options in the NHS for Post-partum Depression, *by Dr Matt Bezeidenhout, London, 2000*), still I felt as though I'd heard a door creak open which had been stuck for a very long time.

I leaned forward and hugged Louisa tightly in what I hoped was a suitably Prue-like posture. All the time, I wanted to prove myself worthy of her by conjuring up the perfect sentence to reassure her she was wrong.

Which was hard, because a part of me still believed she was right.

*

While I've been telling this story, Matt has listened carefully; as if hearing a case study for his finals viva. By the time I get to the end, we are parked outside our house in a resident's bay. Matt reaches out and tucks a blade of two-toned hair behind my ear. I catch a whiff of onion.

'Quite an eventful twenty-four hours,' he murmurs.

I freeze, and feel hot all over at the same time. The memory of airline seat fabric scraping my knees is so sharp it seems to burn my skin. I touch the right one, expecting to feel the betraying ridges of a graze. 'What do you mean?'

'Well, your big meeting, William's birth and now Louisa's confession. Heavy stuff. Reckon we're both knackered. Although I have to say it was fun to be back with the Obs and Gynae guys. I trained with Louisa's consultant, you know. And there's nothing like seeing a new life come into the world. One of life's magical moments. Shame he's so sick.'

'Let's go inside,' I say, sharply, my knees trembling.

*

As I floss my teeth, I think about how life is all about choice. What on earth do you do if you suspect you've made the wrong choice? Or if the decisions you made were the right ones, but based on misconceptions?

Clearly some choices have minimal repercussions. Yesterday, I'd tried on a dress in a bare-bricked boutique on Mercer. The fabric was pink and delicate, with just the right amount of subtle support around the bodice. At today's laughable exchange rate, it was a steal. But still my inner anorexic had balked at sartorial nourishment.

'—and there was something about the cut', I'd said to Matt earlier today, during my severely edited description of my trip to New York, 'which made it far too baggy around the hips.'

'Well, you don't want that,' he'd said, reasonably.

'—and they said they could take it in, and add a few darts here,' I'd said, gesturing to under the bustline, as if Matt even knew what a dart was, 'but I couldn't see the point.'

'Plus,' I'd added, when my last comment had elicited no response, 'the material was really light and floaty, and I know it's been hot here, but it is nearly autumn—'

'Sounds like you did the right thing in not getting it, then,' had been Matt's succinct reply.

There had been a woman in the Club lounge at JFK, reading a book, *How To Bond With Your Child*. In the next chair, her little girl, the mother in miniature right down to the pout, was refusing her Asian nanny's attentions. All three were seeking consolation. And each one, I sensed, was destined for disappointment.

Now, dusk slips through the grass-weave blinds, bathing the walls in fractured light.

'So, do you think I did the right thing, not getting that dress?' I ask, as we brush our teeth.

'What dress?' says Matt, spitting out toothpaste and blood, a colour combination which somehow works for the picture on the tube, but which looks revolting spat into the basin.

'The one in New York I told you about. The one I tried on.'

'The floaty one?'

Very good, I think. 'The floaty one.'

'I thought you didn't like it?'

151

'I didn't say I didn't like it. I said it was too baggy around the hips.' I yank out a long skein of dental floss before remembering that I've already flossed. I try to throw it away in the bin, but it wraps itself around my wrist.

I have to wait while Matt rinses and gargles (*who gargles?*) with mouthwash, a ritual in his night-time schedule as sacred as prayer. His cheeks fatten and wobble with the liquid inside them. *Matt at his most Neanderthal*, I think. 'I said, I didn't say I didn't like it.'

He spits, and then turns on the tap to full force, sluices water around his mouth, before spitting again. Then he holds my gaze in the mirror. His voice is overly even. 'I didn't say that you'd said you didn't like it. It was simply the impression I got after all your negative comments on the dress.' He wipes his mouth dry before hurling the towel into the bath.

'So, you think it wouldn't look good on me?'

'How the hell should I know? I didn't see it.'

'Because if that's what you're thinking—'

'I'm not thinking anything. Why on earth didn't you buy it?' In the mugginess of the bathroom, his tanned brow is speckled with sweat.

'Why do you think?'

Matt frowns, and mutters something I don't catch. 'Look, if this is about you fishing for reassurance that you're worth spending money on, you're out of luck. I'm not in the mood.'

'I'm not fishing—'

'Good, because I can't quite see what buying expensive dresses—'

'It wasn't expensive.'

Matt exhales. 'So, let's get this straight. You find a great dress, which is cheap—'

'It wasn't cheap.'

'Which isn't cheap, but we could have afforded it, right?'

I nod.

'And which is just your colour. And yet you don't buy it. And you talk it down to me, and I agree – even though I couldn't see then, and I still can't see, what the hell it's got to do with me – that you did the right thing, not buying it. And now I discover that actually, deep down, you really wanted the dress.'

I put my hands to my face. 'I don't know if I really wanted the dress, I just want to know whether you think I've done the right thing in not getting the dress.'

Matt coughs a laugh. 'Right now? If not buying the dress has ruined my evening, then, OK, I think you made the wrong decision in not getting the dress. OK?' He strides out of the bathroom, and turns on the television. A football commentator sounds like he's having an orgasm.

I stare at myself in the mirror. Matt's right: it's been one hell of a twenty-four hours. The bags under my eyes are a pair of wrecking balls. In moving to the window to roll up the blind – the better to see these new facial deformities – I trip over the Perspex set of scales. I yelp with pain, and kick them back, which hurts my naked foot even more.

'Now what?' Matt yells over the climax. 'Look, if this is still about the dress, go to fucking Harvey Nichols, or wherever, and buy the fucking dress tomorrow.'

What do you mean: Is this about the dress? I want to ask him. What else could I possibly be upset about? I stand in the doorway, rubbing my stinging foot. 'I can't buy it anywhere else,' I say, tersely, and with exaggerated enunciation, as if to a difficult child. 'It was a one-off piece, from a one-off boutique. New York was my only chance.'

Matt turns off the TV by remote control. 'Oh, what, and I'm

supposed to know that? That deep down you really wanted to buy that dress, despite giving me a very good impression of not wanting it?' He snorts again. 'Well, I took my cue from you. And you know what? You're just furious with me because you're furious with yourself for making a decision, and getting it wrong. And you've no one else to blame.' He points the remote at the TV. 'Any other decisions you've made in your life you want to blame me for?'

And then he switches on the TV once more. The football crowd sounds like it's cheering, just for him.

Chapter Twenty-two

MATT ONCE SAVED my life. For our first Christmas together we holidayed in Cape Town, where the current is fickle, not to say treacherous. We borrowed the family apartment, and sunbathed by day. By night we sipped white wine on the balcony and watched sunsets. In between we giggled over the boys performing one-armed press-ups on the beach, and licked each other's salty skin.

Matt swam like Dad, confident, absorbed. I stayed on the beach, tacked to the towel by a paste of suncream and sand. I would watch him until my eyes ached with the dazzle of sun on water. Deep down, I despised my own timidity.

So, one morning, I waded out behind him and pushed off as he did, mimicking his strong strokes. He was apparently reliving a bunker shot from a game with his father the day before, when he heard close behind him my panting and anxious giggles. Turning, he saw me, my hands little moles' paws floundering in a doggy paddle, thrilled at how far I could swim.

The tide at that hour was shifting. No sooner had we set off to swim back to the beach when I was knocked by the rising swell and dragged under. Panic seized my limbs. My legs flailed in the waxy expanse of icy water. I shouted to Matt, but the wind stole my words. A merciless weight pressed in on my chest. I lacked the strength to scream louder. I couldn't breathe. I needed to raise the alarm, but in heaving one arm out of the water I was sucked beneath the fold of another indifferent wave. Acrid salt water spurted up my nose. I barked several coughs, and my lungs burned. I gasped for air. And all the time Matt was swimming further and further away with every stroke.

What made him turn? When he did, his eyes registered the void where he thought I was. He scanned the sea and trod water, turning full circle in his search. I willed him to see me, but to my horror he now peered back towards the beach, assuming I was ahead of him. *I swim like a stone, remember? Look this way.* Then he turned one final time and glimpsed me as my weary limbs expired and I sank.

When he reached me, he told me to climb on his back. I thrashed out and grabbed his neck. But he soon realised that the current was too strong for him to swim for the two of us. Shocked by his twisting torso and urgent cries to let go, I released my grip and drifted beyond his reach. Suddenly, a wall of cold water smacked me in the face. I gagged and dipped out of sight. The gap between us widened. We were now both gasping, and it hurt our necks to keep heads above water.

Casting around for someone to shout to, Matt saw in the distance, in a parallel line further along in the sea, several bathers. They stood on what was obviously a sandbank, the water barely up to their stomachs. They had a Frisbee and were playing catch, blissfully ignorant of the drama behind them.

'Not the beach,' Matt yelled. 'Aim for those people.' By drifting east with the tide, we could conserve energy. Then he turned on his back and swam, kicking fiercely with his legs as he gripped my exhausted arms, and tugged me to safety.

From the sandbank we walked back to shore as though drugged. Our aching thighs were weak and shaky, our calves stinging. We collapsed on the beach, lying there for several hours, wrapped in towels, holding each other tightly.

Chapter Twenty-three

THE DAY AFTER Louisa's outburst and my row with Matt, I ring the vicar-cage doorbell. In one hand I hold a carrier bag containing a perfumed candle. I've seen them in the lifestyle pages of magazines, and have always wanted one. This morning seemed the perfect time to treat myself.

After a few minutes measuring out the doorstep in pigeon-steps, I walk round the block and push open the garden gate. There I find Dylan in discussions with his gardener – last-minute adjustments for the Harvest Festival fête. I loiter next to the wisteria, inhaling the smell of late-cut grass. When Dylan, who relishes using the Latin names for plants, becomes aware that I'm not a parishioner requiring edification, but a friend prone to mocking his pretensions, he ends the conversation with the hired help and holds out his arms.

'Hey, what a lovely surprise. Are you playing hookie?'

'Not quite,' I say, adding that I've been made redundant. And now, as Dylan holds me, the tears well up which had remained loyally invisible during the morning meeting while the bailiffs took furniture, and while the policeman explained why Interpol is searching for Rex, who has gone AWOL in Spain with all the firm's money.

'Christ!' Dylan kisses my wet cheek. 'What about the famous guy you interviewed on Monday?'

'The bailiffs have taken all the laptops, all the computers.

Apparently Rex has been downloading files remotely. There's nothing left. And we all thought he was a benign old buffer obsessed with reducing his golf handicap.'

'Christ!' says Dylan, again.

Help me, I long to say to him, *like you did once before, by finding me Matt.*

'What does Matt say?' asks Dylan as we enter his kitchen.

'We had a row.'

'About this?'

I shake my head. *About a dress*, I want to say. As if somehow this would make it completely true. I sit down, as Dylan sets about trying to remember how to make tea.

'Hey, you could try being me for a while, and meet the Bishop.'

'Metamorphosis – well, there's a thought.'

'Call it transubstantiation,' Dylan says, making a mess of pulling apart a milk carton.

'So the church really does have an answer for everything?'

'We hate to boast.'

'Well, then, I'll have to try one of those Alpha courses at Holy Trinity—'

'For God's sake, don't do that,' shouts Dylan, flinging cups and saucers noisily on to the table. 'That's not the way at all,' he adds, ripping open a packet of biscuits.

'I was only joking.'

'All right. But really, that's not religion. That's for people wanting easy answers.'

'And what's wrong with that?' I want to know, tugging at my parting.

Dylan spoons fragrant compost into a teapot. 'Nothing, if you're prepared to tolerate the unknown, and endure the fact that not everything has an answer.'

I pull out a hair. 'But there must be meaning. There must be an answer.' I'm almost crying.

'Darling, don't start again. Here, have my – oh no, I haven't got one – here, have a tea towel instead.'

'I thought "God is love" was the answer,' I sniff.

'It is. But not always. There's earthquakes, terrorism, cancer. You can't just airbrush out the bits you don't like. It's all or nothing. Faith is about commitment. It demands full participation. At least, that's what I've been reminding myself lately.'

'A bit like parenting.'

'Yes,' snaps Dylan, as he pours.

'Which makes parenting such a terrifying prospect.' I reach for a custard cream, and nibble its manufactured border. Once the edge is in line with the filling, I dunk it in my tea and suck on its sugary insides.

'I thought the same when I saw Louisa. You know the little fella's not well?'

'No, I didn't,' I say. 'But I'm not surprised. Two months premature.'

Dylan slides to the edge of his chair, stretching out his legs until his body is in a straight line. 'Prue's asked me to perform a naming ceremony tomorrow. Just in case.'

'Ah. She left a message on my mobile this morning, but I haven't got round to returning it. Poor things.' We sit in silence, our hands cupped round our drinks. 'Do you know the worst thing? Everyone'll think I've given up work to get pregnant.' Dylan sniggers. I tell him it's not funny, and he pretends to have been admonished. 'Because, after a time, it'll be obvious I'm not, and then people will start to pity me. They'll think Matt and I are blowing our savings on IVF. Or that one of us is defective. I don't think I can bear it.'

'Bear what?'

'Their misplaced sympathy.'

'They won't think that. Just tell them about Rex.'

I know Dylan's right, and yet I also know it's really my mother, choirmistress to the reproachful, who loiters in the cloisters of my soul, poised to anoint her child with ash crosses of disappointment. And now those massed ranks in the choir-stalls have been joined by Nicole, with whom I had the briefest of conversations this morning in the office, while snaffling things from the bailiffs. She said, only partly in jest I think, that what I needed now, yaar, was a new project – like pregnancy! Just remembering this makes me reach for the increasingly sprouty hairs at my crown.

I interrupt pulling my hair to grab another biscuit. *It's time we all stopped being selfish, na*, Nicole had said, as I held open the door for her. Her words stung me with the force of whiplash. And as I turned to her to say goodbye, it was my mother I saw leaning against the jamb.

Without the structure of my career, I fear I might fall apart. How I long to be brave enough for change.

*

After leaving Dylan to the one o'clock Mothers' Union (which borrows his kitchen of a Wednesday to make copious amounts of Cup-a-Soup, and which he tolerates because it means he gets a free hot meal), I hesitate on the pavement, unsure which way to go. The trees in the street are beginning to shed their plum and golden leaves; they make loud, satisfying cracks when I step on them. From an open window further down the street, I can hear Britney Spears belting out a tune – even she, it seems, is asking to be given a sign.

I walk slowly without any clear purpose, and find myself eventually outside Dylan's church. It isn't all that welcoming from the outside. But it is at least familiar, and I stand for a moment in the porch to consider my options.

Inside, the cool air is dense with a sneeze-inducing cocktail of floor polish, old incense and musty prayer books. I breathe deeply, and make my way to the pew at the front. Ahead of me is the golden reredos drenched in fruity sunlight pouring down from the stained-glass windows. I am meant to find this sight uplifting; to be inspired by the eloquence of God's grace, filtered through human craftsmanship; to appreciate spiritual integration as represented by the Trinity. Instead, I feel I'm fragmenting inside. It's as though my soul is covered with the hairline cracks of the glazes on my father's many pots.

At the opposite end of the chancel step stands the oatmeal and cobalt alabaster statue of Mary. One palm is raised in peaceful greeting. My heart craves absolution, but in that moment life seems too complicated. I feel unworthy. I exist in a moral twilight. By choosing not to have children, I have rendered myself permanently reprehensible. I think of Dad dying, and the man on the plane, my row with Matt, the loss of my job, the renunciation of fertility, my relationship with my mother. Negligible traumas, possibly, in the greater scheme of things, but they leave me with the overwhelming sense that I've let someone down. That I have failed to live up to expectations.

And I remember standing this morning in Fenwick's before a display of candles in glass tumblers. Two shoppers were whispering about them in terms of reverence as the kind of essentials fashion designers took on holiday. *Matthew Williamson swears by them.* Picking one up at random, I ran a finger round its smooth rim. Its

161

purity seemed to burn my sullied skin. I imagined dropping it, surrounding myself with jagged pieces of broken glass, and I couldn't get out of my head the idea of pressing that sharpness into the raised veins at my wrist. *Harper's Bazaar ran a feature on them last month.* Or were they arteries? Artery, vein? Vein, artery? Audio visual, Victoria and Albert. *And that Stella McCartney, she's planning a range.* I could almost feel my skin give a little under the pressure, could almost see the point at which the shard pierced the flesh.

I remove the box from the carrier bag, and undo the packaging. Juniper and lemongrass mingle with the fustiness of embroidered kneelers. I cup the frosted glass and roll it in my palms, anger throbbing through my bloodstream, anger that has been fermenting for what seems a lifetime. I see the elephant pebble arch in the sky and sag towards the sea – can almost smell the rank salty water – and feel deflated. My focus narrows until all I can see is blue. Blue, virginal blue; Mother of God blue. A pulse thumps in my head. My fingers grip the tumbler and then suddenly, after a moment of connectedness, the pressure dissolves and the glass slips from my hand.

Chapter Twenty-four

T O THE NEONATAL unit for William Edward's naming ceremony, laden with carrier bags. I've spent the morning preparing nourishing finger food. Soft textures, easily digested. Yet few of us are truly in the mood for celebration. William is not expected to last the week.

My heart is thumping, afraid of what I might see. I expect wailing and the beating of breasts, such as one sees on footage of Middle East funerals. Instead, the nurses move smoothly between pieces of equipment, adjusting tubes and cables; William's paediatrician stands in the corner, monitoring us all, a father watching over the playroom. He has such a magnificent thatch of blond hair that he seems to be accompanied by his own portable sunbeam. It shines under the halogen lights like an emblem of God's grace. My heart returns to its normal rhythm. This man, whose name tag reveals that he goes by the unbelievable name of Dr Piers Goodchild, seems infallible. His granting permission for this afternoon's christening is tantamount, surely, to faith that William will survive.

As I approach the incubator, Louisa tears her eyes away briefly. Her overgrown fringe is scraped across one cheek. Her smile (with her lips, if not her eyes) is for the doctor, and then she returns to monitoring her tiny baby.

William's wrinkled skin is maroon. He has Ed's hair, apparently, underneath his tiny cotton beanie hat. The thin plastic tube disappearing up his right nostril makes my own nose ache, and I rub at the place.

'Let me take those,' Dr Goodchild says to me, reaching for the carrier bags.

I pull away from him. Like people with a flying phobia who imagine their thoughts keep planes aloft, I want this man to stay focused on William. I ask for an update. Apparently, 'The respiratory distress caused by his immature lungs requires him to be given artificial surfactant to prevent the inner surfaces of his lungs sticking together.' But William has recently picked up an infection, sabotaging this procedure. I think of Audrey having to listen to my father's surgeon, and my sinuses prickle.

And then, just as I reckon things can't get any bleaker, Dylan arrives. And immediately I know that he knows what I've done. My stomach lurches. How stupid to think I could keep it secret. It's almost laughable. All the dips, and snacks, and neat arrangements on the plates, are no substitute for trust. And now witnessing Dylan's tortured face, the beads of sweat on his brow, the dark crescents beneath his eyes, and hearing his weary apologies for lack of punctuality, I am cauterised with guilt.

We ask the doctor to join us after the ceremony, an invitation he accepts with such delight I suspect it might constitute his first social engagement for months. My sweet potato wedges, in particular, receive numerous plaudits, although Louisa eats not a thing. Her parents are trying to interest her in the helium balloons that bob lugubriously around her bed. Suddenly, Dylan grabs my arm and pulls me to the window. His eyes flash, and he whispers with urgency.

'Thank God you're here. I've had a dreadful time. The church has been vandalised in the last twenty-four hours. Nothing stolen, thank God – just loads of mess. The police reckon it's queer-bashing.'

'The police?' My skin flushes. 'Why are they—?'

But Dylan isn't listening. 'One of the churchwardens arrived early to set up for morning prayers, and found— found—' His voice has gone squeaky. He rakes one hand through his ginger curls and clasps the back of his neck, his other hand at his hip, as he gazes out over the view of the hospital laundry. 'It was horrific.' He spits an ironic laugh. 'And do you know who we were due to pray for this morning? The victims of violence. God, it's enough to make you weep.'

'But the police—?' I repeat, touching Dylan's arm.

'Oh, they were fucking hopeless. Apparently, we're not the first in the diocese to be targeted since this whole gay bishop thing caught the public attention. So, no fingerprints, no statements. Now, do you think their indifference could have anything to do with the fact that what we're talking about here is a sexually motivated crime or, more specifically, a homosexually motivated crime? Surely not. They took one look at me and thought, *He can take our investigation and shove it up his arse—*'

The silence in the room is brittle. Dylan half turns from the window and takes in everyone looking at him. Not for him the shame of disclosure. What he sees is an audience! He is back in the pulpit, breaking bread behind the altar, selecting the winning ticket for the tombola. And as he embellishes the details (*it's the first time my churchwarden's had his hands on a broken virgin*), I take the opportunity to slip away.

*

'You left these behind.'

'Thanks for bringing them back, Dyl,' I mumble. I take the plates and resealable boxes, and try to close the front door on him. 'I felt a bit sick, that's all. Bye.'

'Maybe you *are* pregnant!' laughs Dylan, squeezing past me and depositing the rest of the picnic things on the stairs. 'Hello, my darling Tallulah-girl.'

Watching him fraternise with the cat makes my stomach churn. Any resolve to confess my sin to Dylan disappears. After all, if it wasn't for his ridiculous announcement to adopt, I wouldn't be in the free fall I am today. I take the dirty things downstairs.

'That doctor's rather lovely, don't you think?' says Dylan, descending, sneezing loudly. I put the kettle on.

'He's bound to be married,' I retort. 'How could any woman fail to be seduced by the idea of a doctor who cures sick babies? And anyway – you're practically married yourself.'

Dylan sneezes again as Tallulah bolts from his arms and saunters through the catflap.

'I most definitely am not! And he's not, either.'

'Don't tell me. Your gaydar.'

'No, I sort of checked after you'd left. Discreetly. He *was* married, but not any more.'

'There you are, then. He *was* married. That means he's not gay.'

'David was married.'

Ah yes. David. 'Is it me, or are you two seeing less of each other?'

Dylan accepts the cup of camomile and leads the way back up to the sitting room, where he makes for the piano stool.

'It's this bloody baby thing. It's his only topic of conversation. Even when I rang this morning to tell him about the vandalism, he was like "Ooh, and did you see the *Daily Mail* today – they've got a whole piece on celebrity adoptions". And I'm, like, my church has been ransacked by homophobes, I've got the Bishop breathing down my neck and, I mean, what the fuck's he doing reading the *Daily Mail* anyway?'

Dylan spreads an arpeggio across an upper octave. 'God, this is hard. I'm thinking about leaving the church, and David couldn't care less. Not remotely. He wants another child, and that's that. And because my father died so long ago, I don't have any real role models of how to be a dad. I look at Harry and sometimes wonder whether I could be like him, but fundamentally I don't envy what he has.'

Quizzically, I hold his gaze over the rim of my teacup. Dylan thumps down a chord, which makes his curls tremble. 'Well, if you must know, I'm getting cold feet.' More chords. 'About this adoption business.' My heart quickens. 'It was always more David's idea than mine. He has kids already. But I thought, *Why not?* I love him to bits, and it seemed the perfect way to express our commitment. And it might give my mother new focus. You can't imagine how stifling it is to be an only child, the sole object of your mother's adoration—'

I don't remind him that I, too, lack siblings, since in all other respects Dylan's assumption that I *can't* imagine such suffocation is depressingly accurate.

'But let's just say attempts by the adoption agency to discourage you are very effective! And, given our respective ages, we'd be very unlikely to get a baby. Rather, a child from a broken home, someone who has suffered traumas, maybe even abuse. And one parent must give up work completely, at least for the first year; otherwise, they say, what's the point?' He swivels round on the stool. 'So, do you think I should still go through with it?'

I shrug. 'What did David say?'

'About what?'

I roll my eyes. 'About your diminishing convictions. I take it you've told him?'

'You have to be joking!' spits Dylan. 'He never listens to anything I say. Parenting? Dave's got the T-shirt. Leave the church? Yeah, it's just changing jobs.'

'What do you mean, he never listens to you?'

Dylan looks startled. In fact, I think he reddens. 'Did I say that?' Suddenly Dylan seems very young, like a friend at school who has left his lunch money at home.

I wrap my arms around his shoulders. 'How did you and I get to be so alike?'

'Hey,' he laughs, grabbing my hands. 'Maybe you and I should have sex, and then you could have the baby, and donate it to David, and then everybody'll leave us alone!'

'That sounds like my idea of living hell,' I yelp, putting my hand over Dylan's mouth. He tries to wriggle free, but I tighten my grip. He flings me to the floor, and I'm shrieking with laughter. He kneels over me and pins me to the carpet by my wrists.

'Zo! I see. Vee vill haff to haff zee artificial insemination.'

We are gazing at each other. My heart is playing heavy chords in my chest. Dylan is gripping my wrists even more tightly. His face is so close, I can feel his warm breath, can smell the camomile on it. Some of his freckles are larger than others, which I've never noticed before; but then I've never been quite this close before. I imagine the weight of him on top of me. He leans down and our lips meet – his are soft, and seem to merge into mine. And then he pulls away slowly and we are back to looking into each other's eyes. I think he's about to kiss me again, deeper this time, the way a tentative kiss in a film is always followed by something faster, more intense, often up against a wall. Instinctively my insides are aching for that gear change, that moment of ecstasy, and the other part of me, the voice in my head, is screaming: *You idiot, this is Dylan!*

'God, I forgot to say,' he says quickly, scrambling up to sit on the piano stool. 'You've got a part in the show.' And he fans out a couple of arpeggios.

I sit up and hold my breath, so that I don't say anything stupid. I feel dizzy. I have just kissed Dylan. Dylan has just kissed me. And I feel as though he has stepped inside me, taken a good look around and then stepped back out again. All my skin feels alert, unbearably sore. Physically, Dylan still looks the same. Yet when I look at him, the air between us jangles, and he seems blurred somehow. 'What did you say?'

'I said you've got a part in *Company*. Bea telephoned last night.'

I stand up slowly, still light-headed. 'Gosh! Wow!' I try to smile. 'Really? Who?'

'Amy.'

'Amy who doesn't want to get married?'

'Played by Amber who doesn't want kids. It's perfect.'

'You told Bea Whateverhernameis that I don't want kids? What the fuck did you do that for?' Oh Christ, that kiss has destroyed us. I bend over, a fierce stitch in my side.

Dylan holds up open palms. 'Don't blame me. She was asking after you, that's all.'

'She mentioned me?'

'She caught you watching her. During the audition.'

I stand upright again. 'I can't have been the only one, surely? She is barking, after all.'

'Yes, she's used to scrutiny! The deputy head can't make her out at all. It's amazing how often Stanislavsky can be worked into a discussion about classroom refurbishments. But you were looking at her differently, she said. Not out of curiosity or derision. But as if you were sizing her up.'

'What does she know? I thought her area was the stage, not the couch.'

'I think when you've been in The Biz' – here Dylan mimes quotation marks, like David always does, and I feel defeated – 'as long as Bea has, it amounts to pretty much the same thing. She's spent her whole life imagining what it's like to be other people. Apparently, it's one of the techniques she's developed to get to the *biographical truth* of a role!' He raises his eyebrows.

'Good grief. So, what did this thespian psycho unearth about me?'

Dylan starts playing a song.

'Tell me, Dylan. What did she say?' Strident is how I'd describe my voice.

'She said that damaged people see very clearly. That's how they've survived.'

*

Dylan leaves soon after this revelation, to return to the neonatal unit, where he'd left his bottle of sacramental water. He gives me a rushed kiss, a clash of cheekbones; I thought fleetingly it might bruise. I don't blame him for wanting to leave. The atmosphere between us since we were rolling around on the floor has been so pregnant – Christ, no, not pregnant – so awkward, we haven't been able to look each other in the eye. Fifteen years, and nothing like that has ever happened before. Does this mean I fancy him; have always fancied him? Does Dylan fancy me? I feel I might cry, and reach up to press a fingertip to my right cheekbone.

I sit at my piano, and stroke its cool keys. I had a piano when I was younger but, when my parents separated my mother sold it. 'I need more space,' she said when I asked her what had happened to it. The fact that Mother now lived alone in a property that formerly housed three people was clearly an inconvenient inconsistency. She spoke of the sale as casually as brushing one's hair. And I took the absence of any apology or remorse (such as one might offer had one genuinely acted in error) as evidence of my hunch that the disposal was motivated by spite. Part of me hated her for her indifference, and part of me hated myself for having left home and abandoned the piano to its fate.

The telephone trills and I stop playing mid-bar.

'Dylan,' I say, surprised. My heart starts playing a sort of ragtime. What on earth is he going to say? I feel again the warmth of his camomile breath on my face. I want to throw up. And I remember that I still haven't confessed to yesterday's crime; and it occurs to me that Dylan will somehow keep invading my space until I do.

'Amber, I'm still at the hospital—'

I guess William. Oh, poor Louisa. And Prue. What an awful business. Another funeral. We could hold the wake here—

'Amber, sweetheart. Are you sitting down?'

'I know what you're going to say. And I'm—'

'Amber, listen to me. I'm coming to get you.' Thus speaks my dear friend born for the pulpit, the voice of authority and unswerving conviction.

'Now?' I whisper. The tone of his voice makes me want to barricade the house and hibernate for ever.

'Amber. It's not what you think. I've seen your mother.'

It's very tempting in that moment to get all nit-picky, to retort that 'I've seen my mother, too – all my life.' To protect myself behind a wall of flippant semantics. But already I can hear Dylan correcting himself, when he adds: 'Amber, your mother's in hospital, here in London.'

Chapter Twenty-five

BY THE TIME Dylan arrives, I have decided not to open the door. Instead, I sit on the second stair, my buttocks pricked by the sisal matting.

Somewhere deep inside, where I've parked my darkest fears and hoped to have mislaid the keys, there lies the belief that my mother will spoil the things I love. I can't remember when I first felt this way, but all my life it seems I've kept the woman at bay.

Take relationships. As a teenager I listened to my mother speak of boys with a sneer, as if they were feral creatures out to wreak untold misery. Even though her comments were clearly part of a backlash at Dad and his ilk, there was something unpleasantly addled about her condemnation.

At college, I built a new life for myself, away from her; Mother left school early without a piece of paper to her name, never learned to drive, cannot even swim. It's as if her timidity became my lodestar, by providing opposite coordinates. And up until this moment, I thought I'd put sufficient distance between me and my past to be rendered strong and content.

'Are you going to let me in?' Dylan shouts above the swish of tyres from mothers making nifty back-doubles on the afternoon school run.

I know I'm going to have to let him in eventually; to be talked down like a hijacker from the cockpit of my hysteria. Just as, sooner or later, I'm going to have to confess my crime. Dylan knocks again.

On the hall table stands one of my father's vases. I've filled it with the peach roses Nicole brought when she came to Tim's funeral. Their drowsy heads hang heavy over the rim of the vase. I stand, and a petal drops on to the table. I reach slowly for the latch.

Dylan's grave expression shocks me. I expect irritation, given that patrolling a wet doorstep constitutes a very overrated pastime. Instead, standing there in his damp tweeds, he oozes compassion, his head cocked to one side in that concerned way patented by people like Matt.

In the kitchen, tousling his curls with a towel, he tells me how he was strolling across the hospital lobby on his way back from the neonatal unit, reassured to feel the phial of water in his pocket bumping against his hip-bone, when an Indian chap had burst through the main doors saying a passenger had collapsed in his minicab, and could someone give him a hand? While staff sprinted to his aid, Dylan stood next to the information station, which is how he came to be in prime position to see my mother, propelled in at speed in a wheelchair.

As he speaks, I realise I'm holding my breath. London's infamous pollution has suddenly become more toxic.

Dylan fell in step behind the minicab driver, a few paces behind the wheelchair on its way to Casualty. He wasn't sure what made him follow, other than a vague need to keep track. The driver kept trying to assure the medical staff that this incident wasn't his fault. Eventually, after miles of squeaky corridors, my mother was shoved through two floppy plastic panels, which swung back together to reveal a sign barring the way to anyone lacking the appropriate authority.

Dylan was about to return the way he'd come when he felt a hand tugging at his jacket.

'Father. I do no bad thing. See, my card. Good driver. No accident. No 'dorsements.'

Dylan saw that the man was holding out a piece of paper. He took it and, looking closely, found it to be a business card printed from one of those machines found in railway stations. Dylan nodded and then began walking away.

Suddenly he remembered the driver's words, identifying him as a man of the cloth. It was enough to prompt him to turn on his heels and make for the plastic doors. Adjusting his dog collar to full prominence, he flung them open.

*

At the hospital, we gather outside my mother's room.

'She's comfortable,' replies the nurse to Dylan's opening question. 'Still, it's probably best you don't go in. Her heart needs a great deal of rest.'

You seem so sure she has one, I think.

We peer through the porthole. The room is dimly lit. A face the colour of parchment lies swamped by pillows. Complicated breathing apparatus is clamped to the jaw. The lumps in the bed look barely human. I remember bones I saw once as a child at a local Roman ruin – a pelvis and a skull in the dry earth. Those bones were no one in particular, and they mattered only because of what they were in the past.

These bones are my mother.

The nurse rambles on about prognoses. I blank out her commentary, aware of the absence of air in the empty corridor. Not like the bustle and competing libidos in the medical TV dramas Matt and I adore. I glance back through the porthole. Mother's room contains only a bed, a mobile drip and a bedside cupboard.

The nurse is trying to interest me in felt-tipped lines on a graph.

I nibble the quick of my thumb. Maternal recovery is too frightening to contemplate. The rough flap of skin stings as it tears; I suck a droplet of blood. I glance down at the graph paper. Spiky red lines elbow their way up and down the page. They make me want to burst into Mother's room and demand an answer to the question which has haunted me since Dylan's call: *What on earth are you doing here in my London?*

*

Dylan starts the engine, reverses from the parking space, and slots the car into heavy traffic. It has started to drizzle again. Vast grey shapes have appeared in the sky, puffing themselves up with their own self-importance. Leaves fall to the ground in the autumn wind. At one set of lights, a leaf plops on to the windscreen and becomes so ensnared in the wipers that Dylan is forced to get out and remove the fragments now mulched across his windscreen. I am reminded of torn flesh.

We inch down the main road, past the kind of shops that like to imply a higher calibre of seasonal reduction by using signs saying '*Solde*'. Dylan sits with one finger loosely hooked over the bottom of the steering wheel. Kiss or no kiss, I'm just grateful for the way Dylan, the consummate Pol Roger Padre, knows just when to shed his daffy image and assume control.

'I'd like to go to your church,' I say, trying to make it sound as casual as needing a pee.

Outside the vicar-cage, Dylan fishes in his pocket for the key and hands it to me; the police suggested the door remains locked. 'I'll put the kettle on, shall I?'

I nod. And then hitching my coat above my head, I jog towards the building, zigzagging to avoid the puddles.

In the porch, my cold hands fumble with the key in the lock. I pause to blow on my fingers. And looking up, I notice an inscription carved into the architrave: 'Ask and it will be given; seek and you will find; knock and the door will be opened to you'. I feel unworthy of this sanctuary. But some impulse makes me continue. I thrust my hand inside my jumper to give better purchase, and try the lock once more.

The church inside is silent and cold, the air stiff with prayer. Uninviting; but then, I feel I deserve to be shunned. I keep my gaze on the floor. I daren't look around. If I were to glimpse a candle now, a beacon of hope or of unconditional welcome, I'd be finished.

My heart pounds so much that my armpit is sore. With every step away from the west door, I am less sure I want to be here. Part of me dreads seeing chaos, the shock and the shame of it, and part of me dreads finding everything restored. I have so little experience of absolution.

The first evidence of tidying up lies on the stone floor, slumped against a pew. Two corpulent bin liners act as gatekeepers to the nave. A third sack has split. Broken hymn books weep from its wound. The sight hints at hurt and rage and destruction. I ignore the leaden sensation in my stomach and move to the start of the nave. My footsteps ring out on the stone. I move slowly, steadying my breathing. I try to recall happier times – for example, our wedding, when Matt had been waiting for me at the other end.

Then I see them. Tucked into the creases where the pews meet the flagging, I see small chips of blue or oatmeal plaster missed by the sweeper's broom. My head feels light, my knees buckle, and I walk shakily down the rest of the nave by grabbing pew-end after

177

pew-end. I still can't look up, but I sense a flicker of light out of the corner of my eye.

My shoes meet the tapestry runner bisecting the chancel. To the left I come to the iron base of the lectern, and the wooden feet of the pedestal bearing the statue of the Virgin Mary. Each is in its place. Perhaps I didn't—? But then how to explain the broken hymn books—? And fragments of plaster—?

I reach out and trace the column of the lectern. The iron is cold to the touch. And I remember how extraordinarily light it had seemed when I picked it up; not top-heavy at all. Maybe it wasn't the same object— a parish as wealthy as Dylan's surely has several – one for each day of the week, maybe. My fingers reach the gold-plated casing. Then, higher, until my eyes are level with the feet of the burnished eagle resting his claws on a globe.

My mouth is dry as I trace the folds of his wings. And then there, on the left wing, I find what I'm looking for. A dent the size of a grapefruit. And blue paint stuck in the hollow. Flicking it with my fingernail, it drifts down before resting on one of my shoes. I am unable to move, as though the flake has skewered me to the floor. And it's then that I know I must examine the pedestal next to the lectern. A collar of cold sweat tickles my neck, as though a door has opened somewhere and ushered in a gust of fresh air.

The damage is obvious. Deep gouges disfigure the column. Large splinters the size of cigars jut out at odd angles. And the wooden shelf is empty where once stood the Virgin Mary. Only half the ledge remains, with a narrow ridge of cobalt alabaster clinging to the wood. But someone has stood the pedestal upright, in defiance of the rampage. If anything, it appears more holy without its statue. And across the vacuum I can see straight through to the altar.

Someone has replaced the covers and righted the candlesticks. Care has been taken to ensure that any torn cotton is at the back of the altar. In the centre, a candle in a goblet flickers before the cross. *Someone lit a candle for me*, I think, as I buckle to the floor. And, as my knees smash on to the stone, I have an image of myself swinging at the statue with the lectern, smashing the bronze eagle through the plaster, severing the statue from its plinth.

I am vaguely aware of hurried footsteps, of arms enveloping me. A hand strokes my hair. Something tweedy supports my back and I sink into it, with jerky sobs. Tears dribble sideways into my left ear. And a familiar voice is telling me that it's all right, that it will all be all right. Had someone been watching from the choir stalls, they might have mistaken Dylan for a parent soothing a child after a particularly virulent nightmare.

'I'm so sorry,' I eventually croak.

'I know,' said Dylan, still stroking my hair.

I brace myself to withstand anger, but it never comes. After a while, I pull away slightly. 'How did you know?'

He takes a long time to answer. 'I didn't,' he finally confesses. The stroking continues. 'I thought you'd been gone too long. That maybe the vandals had come back. So I ran to find you. And then I saw you reach out to touch the broken pedestal and somehow it all fell into place. You're cold,' he adds, rubbing his hand vigorously up and down my arm.

'I'm afraid.'

'Of what?'

I am trying, I want to say, *to stop myself unravelling*. My emotions feel as though they are spilling out all over the place. I am that sack of damaged hymn books. I think of Matt, and the man in the plane. I think of Audrey, losing Dad, and of me, losing Dad. And how I miss my chats with Nicole over coffee. Tears prickle in my eyes. Another memory swells in my mind.

'You know when we—?'

'What?'

'You know.'

'Oh, yeah.'

'It hasn't—?'

'What?'

'You know. Us—'

Dylan laughs softly. 'Oh my little Bambi-bunny. Why do you always fear everything will fall apart?'

As he takes me back to his kitchen, I feel more settled somehow. Without even realising I'd been knocking, a door has been opened to me, a marvellous portal into a glittering world, rich in the holy grails of empathy and forgiveness.

Chapter Twenty-six

THAT EVENING, Dylan frogmarches me to the church hall for the first *Company* rehearsal. It's the last thing I feel like doing, which is why Dylan has ignored my increasingly outlandish excuses. I resent his smug faith in keeping busy at times of distress, all the more so because I know he's right. At university, I watched, baffled, as he threw himself into the hammam of his social life following aborted romantic liaisons, whereas I would mope around, feeling like a rounding error in the overheads – he practically had to carry me to that pub where he introduced me to Matt.

Tonight he is calling in the chips, making me do his bidding with that practised air of someone used to cajoling parishioners.

*

By the time Bea calls a break, the cast is in shock. An hour spent on just the first forty bars of the opening song (difficult rhythms, multi-part harmonies), and everyone's shoulders have dropped; Julian has vicious cramp in his hands. There are whispers that some of the old guard are planning to boycott the Sondheim and mount *HMS Pinafore*.

'How did we *do* this all those years ago?' wheezes Harry, thumping his chest before biting into one of Serena's flapjacks.

'We were young,' says Jenny, reaching in to Serena's Tupperware tub and smiling as she brings out two flapjacks stuck together.

'And we didn't have work the next morning,' says Clive, wiping fizzy drink foam from his moustache. As he says this, he glances at me.

This is just the kind of sentiment I would expect from a management consultant. Practical, and to the point, and just a teeny bit dull. And then I remember the angular, waxed leg. And how difficult it had been not to reach out and touch it. An image of Clive's airbrushed limbs in stockings and suspenders rears up to revolt me.

'Well, some of us don't have to worry about work, because I've been made redundant,' I say quickly, tearing off a piece of flapjack. 'No, really, I'm fine about it,' I add. Everyone's faces are rouged with well-meaning concern. 'Well, I'm a lot more fine about it than I *was*, let's put it that way!' And everyone laughs, as I hoped they would, so we can drop the subject.

'Well, I think that Bea woman ought to be shot,' says Serena abruptly. 'I don't care if she's Dylan's friend, or colleague, or whatever. She had no right reducing Nicole to tears.'

'She was just trying to instil some discipline,' says Harry, licking his fingers.

'Yes,' I say, 'but there's a time and a place. We are amateurs, after all.'

'"*Very* amateur", she called us. Remember?' says Jenny, picking at the burrs of stray flapjack that have stuck to her jumper. We all nod.

'Well, all except you, my darling,' says Clive. 'You're her favourite.'

Jenny blushes, and reaches into the flapjack tub. 'I've just got big lungs, that's all,' she says, chewing.

'But, I mean,' says Serena, 'fancy making Nicole stand while we were singing—'

'It's all about breathing—'

'Yes, Harry, thank you. I'm well aware of the theories. You think after giving birth to five kids I don't know where my diaphragm is? Or how to breathe effectively? Dylan should have told her that Nicole's pregnant and has just lost her job. She's hardly showing yet, lucky thing,' Serena added.

'What should I have done?' asks Dylan, as he approaches us, his smile too bright to convince me. Serena explains at length, snapping the lid shut on her tub as she does so.

'Well, I— It's a bit tricky you see, because—'

'Believe me,' cuts in Serena, 'there is nothing more tricky than having to function normally when you feel like throwing up all the time, and your back's killing you and your breasts hurt and you just want to curl up and sleep for ever. Can you really imagine what it's like to be pregnant?'

'You know I can't—'

'Right. So don't try and tell me—'

Harry takes hold of Serena's arm and urges her to calm down. The rest of us stand in silence. I've never seen Serena so vexed.

Dylan stares at the floor. 'I just came to tell you that Bea wants Harry, Serena and Jenny for their song. So perhaps we can talk about this another time, eh?' And he turns on his heels.

'She's hormonal,' mouths Harry over his shoulder as he escorts his wife to the piano.

'Does he mean she's pregnant?' I say, almost to myself.

I hadn't meant to engage Clive in conversation. Now that he and I are effectively paired off, I am left with an obscure sense of unease. I stoop to sweep nonexistent flapjack crumbs into my hand, to obliterate persistent thoughts of waxed legs and suspenders.

'I didn't mean to offend you,' Clive murmurs, crouching down beside me. He touches my arm. 'Don't be cross with me. I know why you're no longer working.'

I stand up and, once again, in a silent square dance, his movements echo mine.

'Yes, it's all very odd,' I say, briskly.

'Not,' Clive says, reaching into a carrier bag for two cans of diet cola and offering me one, 'for a woman your age.'

I don't care to reflect on what he means, but I suddenly feel rather hot. I accept the drink, and take a long swig, staring into middle distance, as if expecting to see Rex there, gloating.

'And I'd like to help you, if I may.'

If Clive had been an employment lawyer, I could have understood his proposal; as a management consultant, he's unlikely to be offering me a job. Perhaps he plans to 'define a strategy' or 'devise a rebranding', or whatever it is that management consultants do. I turn. His eyes have an odd glaze to them, and only one side of his moustache smiles. I look away again, barely able to swallow the liquid in my mouth. 'Let me help you,' he says.

'I don't know what you mean,' I say, stepping back.

'Oh, I think you do,' he replies, taking a step towards me.

He stands so close I can see the droop of his eyelids, smell the glucose on his breath. There are droplets of drink on the hairs of his skunk's tail of a moustache. I'd think him drunk, were it not for the fact that he and Jenny are infamously teetotal. I move to place my can on one of the stacks of chairs along the wall, but he grabs my arm.

'Believe me. I'm the man to help you.'

I glance over at the piano. Harry, Serena and Jenny are scrutinising the score. Bea stands with her hands at the place where her waist once was. I shake my arm free.

'And I know what you and Matt must be going through.'

'Don't drag him into this. Leave me alone.'

'It's OK. He need never know.'

I turn to face him. 'What on earth are you talking about?' I can guess, but I want to hear him say it. Or to prove myself wrong – presumptuous, even.

'I can give you the baby you want. That's why you're leaving work. Yes?'

'No,' I reply, coldly. 'Rex has done a bunk with the firm's money.'

Clive ignores my denial. He is smiling. 'It's nothing to be ashamed of. Lots of couples try for years. You and Matt are not alone. I would guess Matt is firing blanks—'

'Clive!' I seethe. This is not the man I thought I knew. 'Shut up.'

'—because, you know, you need someone to make you relax. Matt's a great guy, but hey! Who ever heard of a laid-back shrink?' He laughs too loudly. Maybe he doesn't get much laughing practice in his office.

'Have I missed the joke?' asks Jenny, approaching us.

Jenny and Clive stand side by side, the gap between them the shape of an empty wineglass.

*

Matt is sprawled on the bed, the TV remote on his stomach and his soft penis in his hand. He finds my account of Clive's proposition hilarious. Matt is especially tickled by the idea that he is thought uptight. Somehow the fact that another man thinks he's firing blanks bothers him not at all. Matt knows he's not, and that's the end of it.

I stomp into the bathroom. My husband's quiet self-confidence can be bloody annoying. I want to shake him, and say that his ability to body-swerve might be an asset on the rugby pitch of life, but could he just try to imagine once in a while what it's like being me, head down in the scrum, covered in mud and constantly losing control of the ball. In the bathroom, I slam the cabinet door shut. All the lipsticks inside topple over.

Matt comes to me, switching off the television. I could hear the commentary – his team was about to score an equaliser. 'Heyyy!' he says, and slaps one of my buttocks. Our row the other day is but a mouse's breath in history; Matt has an enviable ability not to bear grudges. He opens his robe and envelops me, and we stand for some time inhaling each other's good scent. Outside, the familiar timbre of Big Ben spreads its tonal security blanket across slumbering central London. He wraps his arms around my naked waist and leans his chin on my shoulder. We stare at us in the bathroom mirror. Matt is tanned, his sandy hair bleached by the sun. I am shorter, and my brown roots are showing. *Isn't it warm? Isn't it rosy, Side by side, By side? Ports in a storm, Comfy and cozy, Side by side, By side?*

Chapter Twenty-seven

MOTHER'S FEATURES hover inches from my own. She is so close I can see the crossed wires of broken veins on her cheeks. Her mouth is a fish gasping for air, opening and closing without sound. I wince.

'Your solar plexus is gritty this morning,' says Ginny, brightly, as she grinds her thumb knuckle into my right foot. The image of my mother is replaced by the sight of my own feet.

'Yeah, well, my life's full of what you might call *grit* at the moment.' *Still*, I think, *pearls are made from specks of grit, aren't they?*

Ginny looks at me wryly. 'And how *is* your mother?'

There's no fooling Ginny. She knows exactly why I've asked for a session outside of our usual routine. I like to think that time spent with her is an inoculation against a particularly virulent disease. Ginny says that my being here is an avoidance tactic.

'Still not well enough to reveal why she was in London.'

This is my major preoccupation. Perhaps Mother is ill, and requires tests unavailable in provincial hospitals. This in turn implies something atypical, or even terminal. Or maybe she's involved in espionage. It can't be shopping – as a child evacuee, mother takes thrift to the point of obsession. The alternatives fly round and round my head. I've not been sleeping. Ignorance is not bliss – it is torture.

*

Mother lies on her back, asleep. A yellowing oxygen mask is still clamped to her mouth. Beneath it her skin is as ashen as clay-slip. I can't help thinking that this is all a charade; that once I've left, Mother will open her eyes, leap out of bed and laugh with the nurses at the practical joke. But this is ridiculous. Not only is she clearly unwell and therefore unlikely to be leaping out of anywhere, but she is not someone I associate with frivolity. If I came home from school with a new playground joke, Mother always made a point of beating me to the punch line; her ensuing smirk not of humour, but of triumph. If I do now remember Mother's laugh, it's because the sound was so chilling, the cackle of Snow White's witch passing off the poisoned apple.

'You can stay if you like,' says the nurse. She reaches under the counter and offers me a recent copy of *Woman and Home*.

'I'll come back later,' I say, feeling as though I've won a reprieve.

*

Bunting, limp from a recent short shower, flops over the front fence. Blurred, photocopied arrows direct people away from the front porch to the garden gate. As I turn the corner, the doleful sound of a single calypso drum slopes over the flint wall.

'Darling. Thank God you could come. I prayed for prolonged rain, but it did no good. The fête must go on!' We kiss on each cheek.

'That is your fate!'

'Very droll. See what daytime fun you've been missing by having a job.'

'I see you've got half the parish out manning the stalls.'

'And half of General Synod has arrived to conduct surveillance.'

The air is filled with the sounds of forced hilarity. Well-heeled retired couples, mothers with buggies, and men in purple shirts: the spiritual elite. Dylan follows my gaze.

'Oh, Christ! The Bish's about to win at Pin the Mohican on David Beckham for the third time. I'm convinced he's working to a system. Could you be a star and escort him to the cake stall. Mrs Beaumont's in a filthy mood because no one's buying her Chocolate Nemesis.'

'And there was I thinking I'd never work again.'

'God will reward you, my child,' he replies, pushing me in the appropriate direction. 'Now, I'm off to don waterproofs for my stint in the stocks.'

'The stocks?'

'A fiver to throw wet sponges at me and the team ministry. It's one of our biggest money-spinners. And I spend the following fortnight in bed with bronchial pneumonia.'

'That's what my mother has—'

But Dylan isn't listening to me. 'I'd pay twice that to throw sponges at David,' he growls.

'David's here?' I ask.

Dylan shoots me a look that says *Don't be daft.*

*

The last child has been hauled in tears from the bouncy castle, trestle tables are being folded, and I am helping boys from the local prep school fill black sacks with rubbish. Dylan is steering the Bishop to his official car, and loading into its boot the numerous carrier bags bulging with prizes.

A spider, abseiling from a branch of honeysuckle, catches my attention. It winds itself down, swaying in the breeze before landing on the tip of a blade of grass. I admire the effort of it all; the unsung heroics of the animal kingdom. God's creatures, no less. It makes me imagine I could endure anything. Or is that just a function of the walled garden, a retreat keeping the chaos of the world at bay?

Dylan approaches, his face framed by a halo of damp curls. He carries glasses of elderflower cordial. Having tested the grass for moisture, we sit cross-legged on the ground. He rips off his dog collar.

'Delicious. Home-made?'

'Courtesy of Mrs Etherington, over there with the paisley kaftan and the Lhasa Apso. She makes it every year. Imagines it absolves her from contributing to the weekly collection plate.' Dylan chews slowly on a slice of lemon. 'And you'll be pleased to hear that the Bishop's finally deigned to fix a meeting. Wound down the window as his car pulled away, as if the matter had only just occurred to him.'

I feel a spasm of guilt in my stomach. In what might be called my current solipsism, I've lost track as to whether Dylan is or isn't leaving the church. 'Did he say—?'

'Nothing. Although he did frown at my latest marketing message on the noticeboard outside the church—'

'Which says?'

'"Jesus Responds to Kneel-Mail". In letters eighteen inches high. Which I rather like. A friend in the States gave me the idea. And I thought, if it's sufficiently reactionary for a bunch of fully paid-up neo-Christian Martha Stewart Republicans, my slightly right of Attila the Hun parish will love it. But the Bishop has other ideas.' Dylan begins pulling at grass.

And when I next stop thinking about my mother, he is saying '—and I'm simply not prepared to become a national martyr.'

Christ, as Dyl would say. I hadn't before thought such elevation likely. And it occurs to me that Dylan has spiked his own cordial with something stronger.

'It's the hypocrisy that gets me. I hoped the Church could be more inclusive. That it could widen its arms to embrace a changing world. But some people don't want to do that. And I know it's my job to be tolerant of them, and of the fact they disapprove of me, but frankly I'm out of my depth.' And he wrenches up a handful of grass.

'I heard on the radio this morning that Bishops in America have agreed to exercise restraint over gay issues, whatever that means.'

Dylan rolls his eyes. 'To avert a split they've agreed not to conse-crate gay bishops or bless same-sex couples. But at what price? Discrimination is still alive and well.'

I finish the last of my cordial. 'But what about people who have sex before marriage? Or who are divorced? Why do only gays get it in the neck?'

'Because we're an ethnic minority historically susceptible to per-secution. Good old-fashioned bigotry. Sometimes I think the church has been hijacked by the Taliban.'

'I think they're scared of people like you,' I say. 'I think change makes people nervous. They hide behind what they know, what they've been taught. Lots of rules, not much thought. But really, you know, they can't hurt you.'

Dylan stops tugging at the grass and rests his hands on my knees. 'And neither,' he says quietly, 'can your mother hurt *you*.'

*

I haven't been at the nursing station a minute when Mother wakes up and calls for water. Before I know what is happening, the nurse, a different one this time, is by my side holding out a plastic jug. It's heavier than I expect and some liquid slops on to my shoes and the floor.

The room is silent except for stray beeps from ominous machines. Their dials glow a sickly green, the room's only source of lighting. Blinds cover the window. I move to the bedside table and pour a glass of water. Then I ask Mother if she's able to sit herself up. It doesn't occur to me to announce myself; that Mother won't recognise me.

A sudden scream pierces the gloom. As Mother screeches that someone is trying to poison her, I feel paralysed, expecting to be told off, and guilty that all the matricidal tendencies of my youth have been exposed. She claims not to know me, but her shrieks are hurled in my direction. Her eyes never leave my face.

She starts to cough, and by the way she shakes her head I can tell she is furious to be so incapacitated. She is almost choking for someone to blame. And looking down at her face I have that feeling I always get in her presence, which is that I must get away.

The nurse hurries into the room and sees me standing away from the bed, a jug in one hand and a glass in the other.

'What's going on here?' she says to the bed. 'Is this how you treat your only visitor?' Before long, she has calmed my mother down. She nods at me to draw up a chair. And, once Mother's breathing has evened out, and the nurse is satisfied that the dials register nothing untoward, she says she'll be just along the corridor, and slips out.

I perch on the edge of the chair, the balls of my palms pressed into the seat. My forearms are locked and my wrists bent backwards. I see the congealed blood where the line is plugged into a vein in Mother's bony hand, and I'm reminded of Dad, and of William, and of how tenuous life can be. I see the wild flutterings of Mother's eyes beneath their flimsy lids.

Suddenly they open, without any flicker of adjustment or recognition. They are calm and blue – bluer than I've ever seen before. They fascinate me, and so I shuffle my chair closer to the bed. Mother is murmuring. I reach for her hand. It feels bony. I want to speak, but my throat is tight. Finally I manage to croak, *It's me.* There's no response. Under our joined hands I see that the crochet of the blanket is unravelling. 'It's Amber.' Still nothing. 'Your daughter.'

Just as I clear my throat to say something new, she appears to focus. Her eyes, now the colour of skies after rain, widen slowly. Mother's grip tightens, trapping the webbing of my thumb.

'I don't think so, dear. You see, my daughter is dead.'

I go completely cold.

'Please hold my hand,' she goes on, her voice now a whine. 'I'm afraid to do this on my own.' And she keeps repeating that she's all alone and very afraid. More worryingly, she then calls out for her baby, and starts to cry. I watch the tears trickle sideways across her cheeks and into the pillow. She closes her eyes.

My chest hurts. And I think back to when Mother would say she wished I'd never been born, and now here she is thinking I really died. And yet I can't move. I am drawn to this strange sight of my mother crying. Not even when she burned the cakes every summer did she ever weep. I sit stroking her hand with my thumb.

Ten minutes pass. And then, just as the smell wafting in from the corridor announces the circuit of the lunch trolley, her eyelids spring open to reveal bitter, black pupils. And I see that familiar look which makes me imagine that the very act of my breathing is unpardonable. I drop the bony hand, as though fearful of contamination.

A porter enters the room, and rattles off the list of culinary options. I wince to hear Mother make lucid, pleasant small talk. The porter heaves her up to a sitting position, swings a bed-table into place, and leaves behind a compartmentalised tray of food. And still she hasn't addressed me.

She cuts methodically into the lamb, and eats it with the potatoes. The carrots she eats on their own; the slice with a speck of parsley on she places to one side. Finally she takes one last piece of potato and pushes it round the plate to soak up the remains of the gravy. She lifts her fork, and turns her head slightly to look at me, and, without using my name, says, 'You can go now'.

Chapter Twenty-eight

S EVERAL DAYS PASS, and I'm back spinning the hospital's revolving door. Outside, an autumn wind tosses empty crisp packets into the air for the hell of it. Despite my daily visits, despite the purchase of underwear and various cotton nightshirts, and making trips to Waitrose to source interesting species of fruit, my gifts and I are always greeted with indifference. The one morning I didn't go, when I had a stomach upset, Mother accused me of negligence.

The Medical Assessment Unit staff are welcoming. They speak highly of the compliant patient in their midst, one content to be prodded and wired up and written about on an almost hourly basis. They don't suspect, as Matt does, that Mother enjoys finding herself the centre of attention.

Although critical of the portion sizes, and the repetitive menus, and of how mealtimes interrupt her TV viewing, Mother devours the cooking and often drops unsubtle hints for seconds. I overhear the nurses tease her that it's rare for patients to gain weight on the unit. Usually they are too weak to eat. *She normally exists on Cup-a Soup*, I want to tell them. *She can't believe her good fortune.* The day following the teasing, Mother is found to be off her food, eliciting further concern from the staff. There is talk of sourcing special meals from the Consultants' dining room.

The good humour I always hear coming from Mother's room dies the moment I arrive. It is irrelevant whether Mother is laughing at some daytime chat show or bantering with staff. The change on seeing me is instant, and mortifying. And I often ask myself why I keep picking at the scab of such humiliations. But every time I step from the Tube and drag myself to the hospital, I see in my mind the moment my mother wept. She'd seemed softer then, almost maternal. Someone with whom I could talk openly, and who would understand.

*

In the car park one morning, I bump into Nicole. She has come for a scan. I hug her for a long time. We haven't seen each other since last week, when Nicole made her understandable excuses and withdrew permanently from the cast of *Company*. Her absence from the political intrigue of rehearsals has left her nostalgic for them. And I miss her, and our chats over coffee. So I am thrilled when she asks me to join her at the scan.

As a column of sun pours in through the window, she and I are already holding hands when the fluttering seahorse shape of Nicole's foetus shimmies on to the screen. From her prone position, Nicole lets out a deep sigh of longing, as if she wishes she could give birth immediately. She reaches out and strokes the black-and-white image on the screen as if it lives inside the monitor. I saw Polaroids of Serena's children at a similar age, but nothing prepares me for the beauty of the quivering image and the amplified watery gurgles. It's a moment to rival television footage of men landing on the Moon.

The foetus weighs as much as half a banana. It has fingerprints, and elbows, and a face. The nurse indicates these places by gently tapping the screen; clearly, routine has not dimmed for her the magic of her job. We laugh with relief at the information, and its implications for health and normality. And the seahorse bobs in time to our voices.

It's as I loiter in the corridor while Nicole supplies a urine sample that I think I see Jenny. Certainly someone very like her, with Jenny's predilection for jolly knitwear. This person is walking briskly in my direction, but is partially hidden by two members of staff. A childish fear of rebuke stops me raising my voice in a public place, but I quickly regret my timidity. I am probably mistaken, and Jenny has always seemed indifferent to children, but I can't let the discrepancy go.

'Oh, hello.'

As we wait for a lift, a man's voice slices through my thoughts. A tall, familiar-looking gentleman with a crest of sunny hair. Of course – William's paediatrician. I introduce him to Nicole, all the while struck by the way he has the size of grip to hold two variety packs of sandwiches in one hand.

But before I have time to ask him about William's progress, Dr Goodchild has got out on the floor below, and I am filled with an obscure form of guilt; that, in not keeping William in my thoughts, he is destined to perish.

And I am struck by how my own existence has lately narrowed. Redundancy, and Mother's presence, have whittled away at my confidence. I haven't learned my lines. I haven't visited Serena and the girls. I haven't telephoned Louisa, or Prue. My shock of peroxide is bleeding brown at the crown. Friends have begun to leave cautious messages, surprised by my lack of contact. Last night we even had to ring for a pizza, for God's sake. Matt had to pop next door to borrow a flyer for the number, since I usually shove them straight in the recycling crate. I then spent most of the evening handing my pieces of cheese-coloured Plasticine to Matt, who seemed oblivious to – no, excited by! – this rare exposure to nutritionally inferior rations.

As Nicole and I pass the hospital coffee shop, I spot a female form draped in garish colours. Unable to persuade Nicole to join me for a quick pastry, we kiss goodbye, and I retrace my steps to where signs indicate 'Fresh Hot Food' and 'All Day Breakfasts', as if the two are not synonymous.

As I carry my tray over to where Jenny sits, I see that her face is drained of colour, even allowing for the café's hostile lighting. *Maybe I should leave her alone.* But it's too late. Something (my hesitation, perhaps?) has broken Jenny's spell and, as she heaves herself back from her thoughts and refocuses on the real world, she sees me. I watch as she struggles to rearrange her features into something more welcoming.

'Hello, stranger,' I say, brightly.

Jenny stays sitting with her elbows propped on the table, clutching a cup between both hands as if she can't bear to let it go. I sense she might want to be left alone, but having been caught approaching the table I can hardly sit elsewhere.

'Heavens, my calves are stiff after all our rehearsing!' I say, compounding the lie with an unnecessary lunge for my leg.

Jenny grimaces, and slurps at her drink. Sitting in the uncomfortable silence, I get the impression that someone has died.

'Do you want to know a secret?' says Jenny suddenly, setting her drink down with such precision that its base overlaps an existing stain. I note the edge to her voice, the exaggerated placidity. It draws attention to, rather than conceals, the sense of someone doing her utmost to remain in control. 'Bea's resigned from the show.'

I lower my cup with such force that it chips its saucer. 'You're joking.' I brush aside my pique at being kept in the dark, since in all other respects this revelation cheers me up. 'I bet Dylan's livid.'

'Dylan doesn't know yet.'

My eyes widen. There are, I know immediately, two dimensions to this scoop. Negotiating the fallout from Dylan's delayed discovery of betrayal will be hazardous, but manageable. Jenny's possession of prior knowledge is, however, surreal and unsettling. The universal order of things has been subverted. And it is then that I suspect that Jenny saw me on the maternity ward, or rather realised that she had been spotted, and that what is happening now is an attempt by her to regain some power. I stick with the subject I've been given.

'Dyl doesn't know? How can he not know?'

'Bea rang me last night. She thinks the cast is hopeless and she can't see us improving. With her reputation, she can't afford to be associated with an embarrassing flop.'

'With her reputation?'

'She's very well connected, Amber. She lives in Primrose Hill.'

'Well, whose fault is it that we're hopeless? It's her job to bring out the best in all of us.'

Jenny starts playing with the grimy funnel of a glass sugar dispenser. 'You don't like Bea, do you?' I frown. 'Well, you don't, do you?' Jenny's eyes remain fixed on the white granules.

'What does she expect? We're amateurs. She knew that when she signed up.'

'But you don't like her?'

'Look, I can't see the point in—'

'Just answer the question, Amber. Jesus! Why will nobody answer my questions today?' cries Jenny, banging the dispenser down on the melamine. The off-duty paramedics poised to occupy the next table make a swift decision to shepherd their trays further away.

I hesitate to speak, since irritability is known to be contagious. On Jenny's cardigan I notice a pulled thread, right there on the chest, as though my friend has begun to unravel from the inside out. As I struggle to work out what this is all about, I remember my mother crying in the hospital, apparently frightened. Perhaps Jenny is frightened, too.

'Can I do anything to help?'

Jenny turns her head away.

'Another drink?'

'Don't leave me here,' whispers Jenny, still looking out across the room.

'Don't worry,' I laugh. 'I can stay all day, if you like.'

Jenny looks back at me, and smiles weakly. Then she stares down into her lap. 'I don't know what to say.' She sounds exhausted.

'You don't have to say anything.' It's one of Matt's lines, and I've always wanted to use it, but it sounds far too wise coming from me.

Jenny looks up. 'Oh, but I do. That's the problem. I've been told it will help if I talk. I've been bottling things up, apparently. But I just can't say—' She looks back into her lap.

'Maybe your words feel inadequate?' I say, remembering how hard I've often found it to make people understand my strength of feeling towards my mother.

Jenny thinks carefully before replying. 'No, not inadequate.' She pauses once more. 'More like horrifically accurate. Deadly, even.'

'That bad?'

Jenny nods.

I shrug. 'So, try me.' I can feel my body tensing up, as I wonder what I might hear.

Jenny shakes her head. 'You wouldn't understand.'

'*I* wouldn't? Or *no one* would?'

Jenny purses her lips. 'I'm not sure.' I'm about to speak when Jenny holds up a hand and continues. 'But don't get me wrong. I'm desperate to talk. I can't bear carrying this all by myself. It's just— you have to promise not to be cross with me—'

'Why would I be cross?' A hot wave floods my body. An awful vision of Matt in bed with Jenny springs to mind. Or Matt and Clive—

'Because I'm such a failure,' Jenny replies, beginning to sob. The sound is wretched and agonised, desperate even, as though vital organs have ruptured; bleeding inside.

And I remember the time, one hot afternoon on a Tuscan stone patio, when I let my friend down, when I sat blistered by her candour and vulnerability, and was found wanting. When I made a promise to myself that I would focus on 'you' instead of 'I'.

I am the failure, I think.

I reach out for her hands, but she has moved them to cover her wet face. So I drag my chair to the other side of the table, the better to hug Jenny's body as it jerks and shudders in grief. The melancholy smell of mothballs, reminiscent of dreams shelved, escapes from the wool.

'This is ridiculous,' says Jenny presently, blowing her nose.

'Don't be daft. It's good to cry. I do it all the time. Matt's always worried because our house is built on reclaimed marshland.'

Jenny spits a short laugh. 'Do you? Cry, I mean?'

'God, yes! Nothing like a good howl. In fact, I can safely say I'm better at it now than I was as a child. Years more practice!'

'Lucky you. I was never allowed to cry. At one of my birthday parties I wept under the dining-room table, and my mum crouched down and hissed that no one had come to see me throw a tantrum. And I wanted to say, *That's the point, Mum. No one has come to see* me *at all.* You see, the other girls in class had accepted the invites simply to eat our food, and call me names, and prod their fingers into my stomach to test how fat I was, saying I was having a baby. I was always told that if I kept my wishes secret when I blew out my candles, then they would come true, but even then I knew that had to be a lie. Nothing I ever wished for came true. I hated my mum for lying to me, and I hated myself for being so miserable. And I've never stopped hating myself. Especially now—' she gulps for air, as fresh tears spill over her cheeks, 'because I thought it's bound to take time, there's no rush— Clive and I got married really young— glad, frankly, to escape my own family— and it would give us plenty of time. Until then we could build our careers— and even when I lost one at seven weeks, I thought there's plenty of time. Then his sister had kids, and then his two brothers' wives. And at family gatherings I knew everyone was looking at me and thinking— and at Clive, which he hated. It was an insult to his masculinity, he said, but I thought we still had plenty of time—' She gulps again, 'And then I lost my fifth – always the same, by week seven or eight— so we had tests— and it's me. I always knew it would be me, and Clive had begun to say so, too— and so we started IVF— needles like knives in my thighs, bruises the size of muffins. I was always so sore— and the cost! And fucking Serena getting pregnant at the drop of a hat, and Louisa. And now fucking Nicole— God!' cries Jenny, shuddering. 'Whose stupid idea was it to put the Infertility Clinic on the same floor as Maternity?'

Another monologue from Jenny once again leaves me reeling. All this time, all these years I've known her, and Jenny has wanted to be a mother. 'I had no idea—'

'Don't worry. We've never told a soul. For Clive, it's a matter of pride, in case people think he's the defective one. It's why he wears that ghastly moustache, you know. Thinks it makes him look more virile. Better that people believe us to be selfishly childless than that he's sterile. For me, it's the sense that it serves me right, that I'm being punished for daring to hope for something good, when I'm fat and unworthy—'

'You're not—'

'I am, Amber. I am. I've always been trying to turn myself into something I'm not. And in this case it's a mum ... By the way, I didn't mean to swear just now.'

'But surely there are other options? Adoption. Surrogacy—'

'Believe me, Amber, we've thought of everything. Clive won't hear of adoption. And surrogacy? Well, that's what today's little bombshell was about,' she finishes, dryly.

'What happened?'

'Well, it's a long story, but we've tried twice, and my eggs didn't take. We were introduced to a lovely woman in Lyme Regis, and I had fantasies that the sea air would work wonders. And the doctors were puzzled, since this woman has two healthy children of her own, so they took tests, and they've finally realised my eggs are damaged. If we'd known that at the beginning, we might not have wasted so much time on IVF; we'd have just implanted someone else's eggs—'

'So, what's stopping you doing that now?'

'There's no money left,' says Jenny coldly, scrunching up her redundant muffin wrapper and depositing it in her drink, small gestures suggesting imminent departure. 'There are so many hidden charges. In the beginning we promised ourselves that we'd do whatever it took. But it takes a lot out of you, you know? And I'm not just talking about the money. So, it wasn't meant to be. That's what I keep telling myself: it wasn't to be. As if all my hopes could be packaged up in that one phrase and pushed out to sea like a ship in a bottle. But then I get to thinking that somewhere out there is my last hope, a woman who will find my ship in a bottle and— Forgive me,' Jenny rises slowly and loops a scarf around her neck which clashes with her knitwear, 'but I just haven't worked out yet how I'm going to let go of my dream.'

I rise, too, and our eyes meet for an instant.

'It's funny,' says Jenny, stooping to pick up her handbag, 'you're the last person I thought I'd tell all of this to. Your life's so perfect, so contained. I didn't think you'd be able to understand how much energy I've expended over the years wishing my periods away.'

I drop my gaze, slightly ashamed of the relief I feel when my periods come.

Jenny's laugh startles me. 'But this is some world, isn't it? You're terrified in case you get pregnant, and I've always been terrified not to. I guess we're all the same deep down, aren't we? Afraid.'

*

We go our separate ways at the Tube. I watch as she heads off into the bowels of the Northern Line. We wave, and she is gone. I change my mind and decide to walk home.

The light is mellow, but clear. Aeroplanes appear purple in the evening sky. My shoes make crisp sounds on the pavement. I feel very connected to this pavement, as though each step is the right one to have made. I feel as though I've had certain gaps in myself filled by Jenny's womanly curves and quiet stoicism. Something inside me has shifted; something almost muscular that I couldn't see before, but which has probably been there all the time.

Chapter Twenty-nine

I RING, AND get Dylan's answer machine. I start a message saying I need to talk to him, and he cuts in, yawning. A minute later, I hear the sound of tea going down the wrong way, followed by lots of swearing. Half an hour later, he is tossing a teabag into a mug for me.

'This is dreadful. First David, then the Bish, and now Bea!'

'Ah,' is all I can think of to say. I smooth down my skirt.

It turns out that, this morning, despite 'lengthy petitions for divine intervention through the appropriate channels', Dylan got the letter (actually just a sentence) confirming his meeting with the Bishop. After days of nail-chewing, Dylan claims he'd cranked himself up to such a pitch, he would almost have preferred it had the Bishop leaped out of the envelope and punched him on the nose. Although I suspect that the part of Dylan's brain still reeling from the best part of last night's bottle of brandy is relieved that this failed to happen.

I notice that Dylan still has sleep creases down his left cheek. 'OK, so I get the bit with the Bish. What's happened with David?'

Dylan groans, and drops Alka Seltzer tablets into a glass of water. 'We've split up. I wish I could say I dumped *him*, but the rage is mutual. But, hey, I'm over it.'

I actually snort. 'So, let me get this straight. You loved David enough to try and have a child with him, and now you've dumped each other, and that's the end of it?'

'What, like, sane and adult heterosexuals don't make those kind of mistakes?' he snaps.

'Sure, we all do,' I say, straightening my shirt sleeves and remembering my flight back from New York.

'Although, of course I was a heterosexual once,' he winks at me. 'For five minutes!'

'Don't!' I put my head in my hands. 'What happened?'

'She was a moose. Enough to turn anyone gay!'

I slap him. 'Not me. You and David. Look, I'm sorry to hear you've split up.'

'No, you're not. You thought he was a twit.'

'I didn't!' I say, slapping him again. 'He just had this whole combat-trouser thing going.'

'Hey, life's a trade-off !' he laughs, moving to sit on the kitchen worktop.

'I just never thought he was as great as you did. But you loved him. And that's why I'm sorry. Because you've been hurt again.'

'If we all stopped having relationships because we're afraid to get hurt, there'd be no point in getting up in the morning.'

'Is that why you're still in your pyjamas?'

'Seriously, the whole baby thing? I'm coming to the conclusion that I got swept up in something, and that on some level it was a way to avoid really looking at my faith.'

I finish my tea. 'What do you mean?'

'I need to make some choices. Decide who I want to be. And it's going to be hard. I have responsibilities. I have a parish. People who look up to me, who want me to do funerals, weddings, these big moments in their lives. And I don't have the answer yet. I'm not even sure there is one answer. But occasionally I just want someone to put their arms around *me* and tell me it will be all right.'

He bangs his heels gently against the cupboards, a little boy who can't reach the floor.

'Which still leaves me with the problem of what to do about Bea. Bitch!'

'Language, vicar!'

'Careful, or I'll make you do it.'

The room is suddenly filled with an absence of sound. A seagull's cry, incongruous in central London, drifts in and out of the silence, as though asking for directions.

'That's it!' cries Dylan, leaping down from the kitchen worktop.

'No—' I groan, sensing the freight train of Dylan's plan careering towards me at speed.

'Yes! You're the perfect person. I don't know why I didn't think of it before.'

'Probably because I'm *not* the perfect person—?'

'You *are*!'

'I can't possibly play Amy and direct at the same time.'

'You've lost your job. You need a distraction from your mother—'

'It's not a great sales pitch,' I warn him.

'Well, what else are you doing with your time? I see you're still wearing your snappy little office clothes and heels, yet I don't hear you mentioning interviews.'

I am momentarily stung. Can't he remember how lately I've been struggling to hold it all together? Or how I lashed out at the mother of his church?

'Well?'

'Sorry. My mind's on other things,' I say, standing up.

'Please, Bambi. Please do it for me. It'll get me out of the most frightful hole.'

His use of my pathetic nickname only hardens my resolve. 'Sorry,

Dyl. I've got rather a lot to sort out right now.' But, knowing that he'll badger me until I give in, I start talking about my mother, and the fact that she seems afraid of something. Or someone.

'So, you think she was in London to meet someone?'

'It's possible, isn't it?'

'But you've asked her, surely?'

Historically, I remind him, the relationship has not permitted such freedom of expression.

'Good point. So, ask the taxi driver who drove her to hospital. He'll know where she was headed before she was taken ill in his car.'

'Right. I'll trawl through the list of twenty thousand unlicensed cabbies in London and miraculously find the guy I need. That should keep me busy for, what, half an hour?'

'Now, now,' says Dylan, striding out of the kitchen. 'Don't be tetchy.'

I drop my dead teabag in the bin and return to the table. I watch as morning sunbeams filter though the oak tree in the garden; the dust motes inside them are doing pixie dances on the kitchen cupboards. When Dylan returns, he is wearing a tweed jacket over his pyjamas, and a self-satisfied grin on his face.

'Very fetching,' I say, tracing whorls of wood in the table.

'What a shame you find my latest attire so, how shall we say, tiresome.'

'If the Bishop doesn't sack you for heresy, it'll be for sartorial schizophrenia.' When Dylan fails to reply, I look up to find him holding something out to me. 'Where did you get this?'

'Keep up, Einstein. It's been in my pocket all the time. Since your mother was admitted.'

'But why didn't you tell me?'

Dylan flops into a chair. 'I withheld it deliberately, because I am spiteful and childish,' he intones with feigned sincerity.

'OK,' I say, penitently, stroking the driver's business card. 'Even *I* didn't know this might be useful—'

'Even you!' retorts Dylan. 'Even Little Miss Perfect!'

I lean over and kiss his cheek. 'Oh, Dyl, this is brilliant. I'll ring this guy as soon as I've seen my mother. In fact, I might even ring from the cab.' I start gathering my belongings. 'This is the best news I've had in ages. I don't know how I'm ever going to thank you.'

*

My first act as the new director is to force Dylan to offer Pamela a role in the rejigged cast. This Pauline conversion is achieved by persuading him that a better show can be achieved at very little cost to his sanity. Privately, I hope to exploit his mother's hoarding tendencies for costumes and props. Whereas I loathe clutter (my monthly donations keep numerous local charity shops financially solvent), Pamela stockpiles everything, as though early widowhood rendered her incapable of losing anything else. If the production's a flop, at least it will be visually authentic.

After a fleeting visit to the hospital, where Mother informs me that she's 'never liked this particular brand of chocolate', I drive to Kentish Town. Over a midday gin and tonic, Pamela agrees to play Joanne, the blowsy, ageing alcoholic who inadvertently gets the hero to consider marriage. Pamela's fun, but she is exhausting. Her ready supply of waspish anecdotes always has me feeling I'm auditioning for something.

'So, do you plan to remain in headhunting?' she asks sharply, at one point.

I murmur something about having a few things to sort out first.

'Ah yes, your mother,' says Pamela, crunching on an ice cube.

Dylan is so bloody indiscreet.

'Well, there's so much about my mother I don't know. What was it someone once said? "The unexamined life is not worth living"?'

Pamela lights another cigarette, shakes the match and inhales deeply before locking her eyes on me. 'I prefer to think that the unlived life is hardly worth examining. You'd do well, dear Amber, to remember that, before you waste your life trying to change what cannot be changed.'

Chapter Thirty

'IS IT OK if I leave my car outside?'

The man I am talking to sits in an old swivel chair. Its red leather is cracked, and it squeaks as he pushes at the wall with one of his slippered feet. On the wall, there hangs a silver tinfoil frame surrounding a portrait of the Hindu elephant god, Ganesh; Nicole had one in her office. This one winks in the flicker of fluorescent lighting. Precisely measured vowels flow from a transistor radio on the counter. The man is listening to the lunchtime news on Radio 4 and jotting down words in a notebook. I repeat my question.

The size of the kiosk, identified outside as Vasant's Vauxhall Vehicles, means that no sooner have I crossed its threshold than I have reached the counter. The man I assume to be Vasant lurches out of his chair and turns off the radio. The fierce crackle of two-way static scrapes the walls. He apologises for not quite catching what I said. I am aware that he speaks slowly, carefully even, but with beautiful diction.

'Will my car be OK there?' I repeat, turning to point to where it rests half-mounted on the pavement. 'I've left my hazard lights on,' I add, as if this will clinch it.

The man nods. 'Double red. Wery bad. Wery bad indeed.' He looks at me quizzically, as if trying to work out who would drive to book a cab. 'You want a taxi?'

'No. I wish to speak with Mr Vasant Deva. I telephoned earlier. It's a private matter.'

211

'I am Mr Vasant Deva,' he announces, with an engaging tilt of the head. 'How may I be of serwice?'

'Well,' I say, 'first of all, what shall I do with my car?'

Vasant suggests we sit in my *vehicle*. I am sceptical, but his references to the dearth of parking options, the lack of temporary permits and the officiousness of traffic wardens settle the matter – as does the way he accompanies his monologue with locking up the kiosk.

We've passed only one set of traffic lights before Vasant tries to get out of the moving car. 'It wasn't my fault. I'm a good driver,' he cries, struggling in vain to override the central locking system.

I pull over. 'Stop that. I'm not the police. The woman I'm talking about is my mother.' Vasant lets go of the door handle. 'I want to find out where she was going the day you ended up taking her to hospital. I thought you might remember.'

'Where she was going?' His eyebrows wrinkle. 'She was going where she always goes.'

I suppress a small cry. 'You've driven my mother before?'

Vasant appears to be trying to press his spine deeper into the passenger seat. 'Many times,' he replies, cautiously.

A cold chill sweeps my body. Mother has been in London *many times* and I've never known. 'How many times?' I say, trying to stop my insides from feeling as though they want to explode.

Vasant has no idea, in the sense that the arrangement has been going on for over ten years. He was driving one day near Vauxhall station, when a lady standing at an empty taxi rank stepped into the road and waved him down. He drove her where she wanted and, as she got out, she asked him to wait. At the end of her return journey, she asked whether she might contact him again for similar future journeys, and he agreed, for it had been pleasant to spend the afternoon 'in the suburbs'.

She would telephone the kiosk perhaps a day or two in advance. Even if one of the other drivers took the call, it was Mother's preference to be *escorted* (that was the word she used, apparently) by Vasant. Some of the cabbies would tease him about his 'bit of skirt', but he never rose to the bait.

For the duration of their first journey – apart from her requests top-and-tailing it, so to speak – not a word passed between them. Yet over time a pattern evolved. Complete silence was confined to the outward journey; if she spoke at all, it was on the return that she would become marginally more talkative. On one occasion, Vasant had ventured a comment of his own (on an enforced diversion into Earlsfield, if he remembered correctly), but she had not taken him up on it. And, in truth, Vasant preferred her soliloquies. It was, he told me, like enjoying an afternoon play on the radio. Once or twice (but only once or twice, he stresses), he had watched her in the rearview mirror take out a hankie and dab her eyes.

Vasant agrees to come with me and give directions. Which is lucky, as I can barely see to the end of the bonnet through my tears.

*

My limbs feel heavy. I am ready to give up. The woman in the porter's lodge, whose badge pinned to her cardigan identifies her as Antonia, is being as helpful as possible, emptying every box file, every drawer. But between us we lack the necessary information.

'I'm so sorry, pet. I need a date,' says Antonia. *Like Anthony*, I think, *the patron saint of lost things*. She sounds so genuinely keen to help me that I soften inside a little, as though her compassion will see us through. 'I just can't do a search without one. Otherwise, it's the old needle in a haystack!'

She and I are both shivering in her draughty room – a workman is repairing a vandalised latticed window. Wind whistles through the gaps, disturbing piles of papers.

I run back to the car, where Vasant is listening to what sounds like an instalment of a Wilkie Collins adaptation. He winds down the window and a breath of warm car fug brushes against me. I remember the Ganesh picture hanging in his kiosk, and I say a little prayer. Then I bombard Vasant with questions: Did Mother ever mention a date? He's not sure. What kind of date? I give him more detail, quoting Antonia. Suddenly, his face lights up. From his pocket he draws out a small notebook, the one he was scribbling in when we first met. He consults its pages carefully.

Armed with Vasant's information, I race back to Antonia's wind tunnel; the gravel beneath my shoes gives off a satisfying scrunch. After a brief flick through the appropriate leather-bound tome, Antonia locates the precise coordinates. She comes over to me beaming, removes her glasses, and gives me an enormous hug, rubbing my back. Then she leads me to the doorway to point out where I must go.

The copper trees lining the paths rustle in the wind. They sound as excited as I am. After a few minutes, I get to an informal T-junction in the gravel. I spin round to find Antonia still standing in the doorway, pulling her cardigan around her. She waves energetically, and signals left.

I set off along this next path, a fist squeezing at my heart.

Chapter Thirty-one

WHEN I WAS a child, I had hoped I was adopted. Attempts to carbon-date the moment when I hit on this notion are for ever linked with the grey of my parents' bedroom, before I started school.

'Don't ask stupid questions,' Mother replied from her bed. (The phrase 'Your mother's just having a lie-down' is one of my earliest memories. My first mimicry of this line earned me a wallop, but the stifled giggles from the greengrocer made it worthwhile.)

It wasn't just that the idea would have led to fantasies as to the fairy-tale lives of my true parents. It would also have legitimised my early ambitions to escape.

*

Mother is being discharged today. Dylan has dropped me *en route* to meeting the Bishop. I've decided not to drive. Of the two possibilities (that my failure to provide transport will be viewed as typically thoughtless, or that my offer to drive Mother home will be rebuffed), I prefer the former. Maybe I endure my mother's contempt because it is less shattering than outright rejection. Her corridor greets me with the smell of bleach.

Mother sits at the foot of her bed, talking to a male nurse I do not recognise. She wears an oatmeal-coloured jacket with matching slacks; the outfit, presumably, from the day of her collapse. I have never seen her look so smart, so coordinated. Beside her in a neat pile lie all the new clothes I bought her during her stay. The nurse excuses himself.

'Agency,' whispers Mother, arching her eyebrows. I feel as though I am expected to concur with the implied insult.

'Shall I get you a bag for those?' I ask, nodding at the clothes.

'No. I'm leaving them here. They're not what I would buy,' she adds.

I let this pass. I cross to the window and look out at the river and the Houses of Parliament. A police motor launch bumps against the tide, doggedly in pursuit of something.

'You don't have to stay,' says Mother. 'They've organised a car to take me home.'

'All the way? It's over seventy miles.' *No wonder the NHS is over budget*, I think.

'I can't manage on my own. What with all the equipment I must take.'

I turn around. 'What equipment?'

Mother gestures limply at a black oblong box on wheels against the wall. I go over to inspect it. It has dials, and a corrugated tube connected to a grey mask.

'What's it for?' I can guess, but having established a base camp of neutral conversation I don't want to aim for the summit too soon.

'Oxygen. The bronchial pneumonia has left me very weak—' I hear pride in her voice, as though she has reached the next round in a national competition. '—and I need help breathing. I can use it during the day, but it's mainly to wear when I'm asleep. Not that I intend to.' Mother's back appears to ripple. 'So, as I say, the unit's very kindly arranged a car. It's nice to feel that someone cares, at least.'

I make a conscious effort to resist the familiar bait, but 'I can't imagine you'd've wanted *me* to drive you all the way to Sussex' blurts out. I want to slap myself.

'Of course not,' says Mother, sharply. 'Don't be so stupid.'

I take a deep breath. 'I'm not stupid,' I say, more evenly. 'I am merely pointing out that you'd've loathed the trip as much as me.'

'Don't pick me up,' says Mother, quickly. 'It would have been unbearable, because you're always so cold.'

'Only with you,' I say, in spite of that mantra in my head telling me not to get involved.

'You always were a secretive child,' Mother continues, 'rehearsing your little plays. You never even cried in the night as a baby. You were so self-sufficient.'

There is a soreness at the base of my neck. We have never talked this way before, and I'm not entirely sure I am happy with us talking this way now. All the same, I feel unjustly accused. *And why do you think that was?* I long to say.

For the first time, she turns to look at me. 'You have no idea, have you, what it was like watching you with your father? To see the way you played with him and not with me. When you came home from school, you used to race to his studio and sit fumbling with clay. For hours! What did you find to model all that time? It's just pieces of baked mud. I just don't get it. Do you have any idea how much that hurt me?'

'I was just playing, for God's sake. I was being a child.'

Mother's eyes flash with anger. 'You took him away from me.'

I stare at her, astonished. 'But you and Daddy shouted all the time. He left us.'

Her eyes narrow. 'Yes, you've always blamed me for that. But where were you the evening he left? Flounced out to a party, as I recall. Came back and bragged that you'd started smoking.'

217

I cross over from the oxygen tank and sit down on the bed beside her. I look down at her bony hands and think how simple it ought to be to reach out and take them in my own, and how sad it is that I can't bear to touch my own mother. Before I know what I'm doing, I've tucked my hands under my thighs. Pity I didn't think to do the same with my tongue.

'Actually, you're not the warmest of people.'

At this, Mother stands up abruptly and starts pacing the room. 'What an extraordinary thing to say. You were fed, weren't you? Clothed? Your father was devoted to you. I wasn't aware I'd been such a bad mother. But now I know that this situation is one hundred per cent *you*, and nothing to do with me—'

The agency nurse appears in the doorway. The car is running late, he tells us with an apologetic grin. Could he get us cups of tea? We both quickly shake our heads.

'It's a result of your behaviour, because of how *you* were,' hisses my mother as the nurse retreats.

'Well, there's a context for everything, and mine is that I was raised by someone who was very closed off. I'm a product of my upbringing just as you're a product of yours.'

'How dare you presume', seethes Mother, striding to the bed, 'to know about my upbringing. You don't know anything about my upbringing—' She towers above me, the lines at her lips standing to attention.

'And you accuse me of being secretive!'

'You were too young. You wouldn't understand.'

'You say that as if you can't believe I'd understand *today*.'

'The world's a brutal place, Amber,' Mother declares. 'One will always be betrayed. When my parents died in the war, I had nobody to help me. I was out of London, and my carers couldn't have cared less.' I watch as Mother reaches up her sleeve for a small lace hand-kerchief and uses it to blow her nose. Its delicate fabric makes me feel warmer towards her.

'And you were very afraid—' I say, moving towards her.

'Don't tell me what I did and didn't feel,' she snaps, shrinking away from me. Her eyes are bright and sharp. 'You're jolly lucky I'm not the sort of woman to roll around on the floor—'

'But that's what I've been trying to tell you. It's very hard to be the child of someone who's so buttoned up.'

'Oh, really. Then I can't wait to see how yours turn out.'

I take a deep breath and turn back to the window. The old buildings stand tall and strong across the water. A lone buoy bobs in the current left by the police launch. 'I'm not having children. That is, we aren't. Matt and I.' I bristle. Even this disclosure feels irresponsible.

'You never told me,' says Mother, the words like pips on her tongue that she spits on the lino.

'I'm careful never to tell you anything,' I mutter under my breath, appealing to the House of Lords.

'But I've always wanted grandchildren.' I turn in time to see her move slowly, reaching out for the bed before sinking into the mattress. Her eyes are fixed on her shoes, as though she might find my babies playing at her feet.

'But you told me once you didn't *like* children.'

When she speaks, her speech is slow, as if she's trying to remember. 'I said that? When?'

'When I was little. I think it was your way of treating me like an adult. Can you imagine how I felt when I heard that?'

When Mother looks up again, it's to ask me why I'm not having children.

'God knows,' I sigh. 'Because of all this, maybe? As I said, you told me you didn't really like children.'

'Oh, so it's my fault?'

'No, I'm not saying that.'

'So, what are you trying to say? That I should have provided you with brothers and sisters for you to practise on? That this is your revenge for being an only child?'

I have a knot in my stomach. 'But there was another child, wasn't there, Mum?'

'This is stupid—'

'Vasant took me—'

'Vasant?' she screams, rising. 'How dare you!' She leaps for the doorway. I've never seen her move so fast. 'When's that car coming?' she yells to the empty corridor. I sit on the bed and watch her dart back and forth. 'This will have huge reverberations,' she announces, before running back out into the corridor. When she finally returns, it's to the armchair, where she sits clutching its armrests. There is a silence before she speaks again. 'I don't think I can bear sitting here with you until the car comes, so perhaps you'll be on your way.'

I hear the familiar strains of Mother deciding what is best for both of us. I slide off the bed and stand alongside the chair, gazing out over the river, tugging at the hair at my parting. The police launch is now heading back the way it came, gliding by beyond the double glazing. I have the impression it wasn't successful in its mission.

'I always thought it was my job to make you happy,' I say, my words on the pane of glass becoming spores of condensation. 'But, because you were always so miserable, and bitter, I guessed I'd let you down.'

Mother is silent for some time. When she finally speaks, her voice is completely flat. 'I think your father had the same idea – that he could turn my life around. That he could spin me on his potter's wheel and create a happy woman, like one of his vases. I've always suspected he married me out of pity. And that made me contemptuous of him, that he could have been so noble and warm-spirited towards someone like me.' Her eyes light up. 'When we were first married, he'd sketch me. Those drawings made me feel special – whole again, somehow. But then you came along, and he took to sketching *you* instead.' Her mouth is set rigid.

I feel things clicking into place, like reading a perfectly crafted sentence. 'But that doesn't mean Dad stopped loving you.'

'Believe me, Amber,' Mother says, sharply. 'You have no idea. No idea about anything.' Mother's gaze is fixed on the squares of lino. 'Wretched was the word they used about me.' She folds her arms across her chest. 'I never dreamed I'd tell anyone this. I never even told your father, I was so ashamed. I wanted my parents to stop thinking of me as wretched. I was so sorry for what I did that, when they told me I must leave London to stay in a home— It meant being alone at the birth, but I was prepared to do anything to earn their forgiveness.'

I crouch down on a level with her knees.

'I hadn't meant to disobey. The Common was out of bounds, they said. It was so visible from the air, it made the perfect landmark for German bombers. And what with being so close to the river and the docks, it wasn't considered safe to even play there, let alone walk home across it. But I was tired, and it was about four o'clock. Dusk. So I took the short cut home— And afterwards, I felt so guilty. I couldn't tell anyone what had happened.

'And later, when I began to show, my parents changed their mind

221

about keeping me in London. I was never an evacuee like other youngsters. I wasn't sent to a family, but to a home for fallen women, to be punished for my indiscretion. I never even got to finish school.' She pauses. 'I've thought about their decision all my life, and now I think perhaps they were also punishing themselves, for not being able to keep me safe.'

Cramp forces me to shift position; to kneel. Mother half turns at the adjustment and looks at me. There are tears massing in her eyes.

'So, you see, love is very fickle. It's turned on and off like a tap.' She looks away again. 'They never came to visit. Of course, I thought that when they saw my baby they would love me again. That they'd see I hadn't meant to hurt them. And then they were killed in a raid on Battersea, and they never got to see her—'

My mother weeps. It is an uncomfortable sight, not least because it's as though she doesn't know how to do it. The water that swells her rheumy eyes is stopped before it has a chance to become tears. She weeps in the manner in which I guess she has grieved in private for decades, taking care not to tear again the fragile fabric of her life.

'And I knew then that their deaths were my punishment for— you know—'

'For what? For getting pregnant?'

'I was raped, Amber!' she cries. 'Raped in a place I'd been forbidden to go to. How could that *not* be my fault?'

My muscles tighten and I hear a rushing sound in my ears. The walls of the room appear to contract around us and dilate again, in constant waves of horror and messy understanding. It quite chokes me, this pain of remembered pain. And, almost blindly, I reach out to grab at the rigid balls of Mother's clenched fists.

'God sees everything,' Mother cries, yanking her hands away.

'How often have I told you that? God saw me that day and sought to punish me.'

I am shaking my head.

'When the matron at the home told me about my parents, I didn't speak for a week. And then the baby started coming. I knew it was too early, but there was nothing I could do. I gave birth to her all on my own. My own, my little baby. I never got to hear her cry.'

And suddenly Mother creases over and howls into her lap, slashing my wrists with hot tears. Occasionally, phrases seep out from under her hair, wretched spasms of rage and loss, about her parents, and being forbidden from holding her daughter before she died. But most of the time she simply repeats one word over and over again: *June. June. June.*

*

'I suppose now you've heard all that, you'll want to sever connections,' my mother says, once she has composed herself and tucked the handkerchief back up her sleeve. I am not thinking that at all, but she is already on to her next point. 'I'm sure I made mistakes. But you'd do well to remember, Amber, that in a family there's always a parent who gets it wrong and a parent who stands by and allows it to happen.'

I dig my nails into my hand and will myself not to retaliate. For I realise that marriage, parenthood, divorce, widowhood: none of these has defined her as much as her wartime losses. And that I am as much to blame as she is for our dreadful relationship. Change, if it comes at all, will be partial, and will require a dropping of guards on both sides.

'I like the name,' I say lamely, trying to be generous and finding it awkward. And suddenly I remember Mother's botched efforts to bake a cake every year in June, and my eyes fill with tears. I wipe them away with my sleeve.

'Do you?' says Mother, smiling. 'I've always loved it. My Junie. In naming her, I made her mine. Without a name it was as if she'd never existed. The home didn't offer baptisms for bastard babies, let alone dead ones. The wardens considered such quaint practices superfluous. There wasn't even a funeral.'

'And I thought the gravestone was nice.' This isn't quite true. It certainly isn't what I would have chosen, but then I've never needed to make such a choice. Mother did. And I can see that this makes it the right one.

'Did you?' says Mother, suddenly wistful. 'It's not the real grave, of course. I read about it in a magazine. About the importance of having somewhere to go to focus one's grief. So I chose a cemetery near Clapham, where she was conceived.' She turns to look at me, her living daughter. 'There hasn't been a day when I don't think about her, want to reach out for her. And now there's a grave for me to visit. Something of hers, with her name on it.'

'Ah, Hope. There you are.'

We both turn in the direction of the door, where a porter's presence fills the frame.

'Your car's here. I'm to take your things.'

I rarely think of Mother as having a first name. In fact, I realise now, I rarely think of her as a proper person at all. She is 'Mother', a label laden with bad memories and contemptible connotations. Long ago she was born, and given a name. And yet, over time, as more and more things slipped from her grasp, it was as though Hope took it upon herself to shed her own name, sliding into a black hole of hopelessness, and effacing all her attachments. Now, for the first time, I think I might have to try to integrate, in my own mind, the two women into the one person.

And I am reminded of the stained-glass triptych in Dylan's church, its three separate windows telling one story. I stood before them when I took my marriage vows; they gazed down upon me during my rampage; would gaze on me still, were I ever to return and kneel before them, seeking forgiveness from their bright chips of dazzling colour. And the thought of them, of their glory, of their unspoken benevolence, overwhelms me with conflicting feelings of longing and trepidation.

*

Little of consequence is said in the lift. Outside, the autumn breeze has died down. Neither of us tries to account for what, if anything, has taken place. I think we both know it's too early to say.

Yet, in the car park, as the porter strains to heave the oxygen tank into the boot of the car, we both make tentative suggestions as to possible future meetings, in an attempt to dilute the imminent ending. I look at her, in her plain oatmeal suit, and I see an old woman who has been lonely for most of her life, and whose daughters couldn't change that.

'Have a safe journey,' I call out, as the driver starts the engine.

Suddenly Hope winds down the window and reaches out to grab my arm.

'The ring.'

I frown as Hope's bony fingers dig into my flesh. 'What?'

'The ring. I threw it away. I'm sorry.'

'What ring?'

'The amber ring. I threw it away when your father left. My

mother's ring – the one you're named after.' She is having to shout above the noise of the car. 'So I have nothing to leave you. Forgive me.'

I stand still, not knowing quite what to say to this; I didn't even know she had the ring. Mother's expression is impossible to read. If it ever *had* been. A discarded plastic cup turns a small pirouette and bumps into my shoe. And as I glance down to kick it aside, I sense the car pull slowly away, and my mother's withered fingers loosen their grip, stroking my wrist as they do so before fluttering softly, swiftly, out of reach.

Chapter Thirty-two

NEARLY EVERY SEAT in the church hall is filled. There is a low buzz in the room. Peeping through the side of the velvet curtain, I can see people chatting, reading the programme, unwrapping sweets. Nicole and Dominic walk down the aisle. They've spotted some friends and have stopped to talk. Nicole absently strokes her gently swelling stomach; Dominic is looking around for somewhere to sit. Matt, sitting next to Audrey, raises an arm and waves, to indicate the seats he's been keeping for them. In the third row I see Vasant, whispering to a lady in a sari, presumably his wife. I am relieved to see the audience looking relaxed, but this doesn't stop me feeling faintly sick. I glance at my watch.

I turn and cast a quick eye over the table of props in the wings: a black shoe and a tin of polish, a box of brownies, a cocktail glass. All perfect. But the cake! Where is Amy's cake for the first scene? Panic swoops into my stomach.

I squeeze myself round the table and sprint past the flaps to the back of the stage. Sixth-formers from the school where Dylan is a governor are repositioning a sofa in the middle of the stage. In the corridor, above the sound of Jenny warming up her voice, I hear footsteps and heavy breathing. Serena appears, half hidden by two tiers of wooden cake complete with a circle of fake candles on top.

'Sorry,' she says, handing me the cake, and bending over with a stitch. The cake is as heavy and as awkward to hold as it looks.

'Harry left it at school. The woodwork teacher says if it's not right he'll make a smaller one for tomorrow.'

'And where's Harry?' I say.

'In the loo, gargling with TCP. He's picked up a bug from the girls – they've all got colds.'

'I can't do up my cuffs,' yells Dylan, rushing up to us and holding out his arms. 'Can one of you do up my cuffs?'

Serena obliges, and murmurs words of calm.

'Beginners, please. Three minutes,' says Julian walking past, followed by the ten members of the church orchestra. He's made them all wear black tie. I want to kiss him.

'Oh, God,' groans Dylan, 'that's all of us. And my mother's not even here yet.'

My jaw clenches. 'Your mother's not here?' I say. I drag my hands through my hair, forgetting that part of my costume includes a short bridal veil. Hairgrips clatter to the floor.

'Joke!' trills Dylan. 'I'll go and get everyone on stage.'

I close my eyes and take a deep breath. Some people have dreams that they are about to sit a maths exam; others, that they're in an interview, naked. My one recurring dream is that I am on stage and haven't learned my lines, and must keep slipping into the wings to re-read the script.

Jenny is first up from the parish hall kitchen, which is doubling as the female changing room. For the first time in months she has a sparkle in her eyes. She helps me re-pin my veil, and I give her a quick hug; her floral perfume is warm and soothing. Clive leads out the men – variously, they are tugging at jacket sleeves or massaging throats. The orchestra is tuning up.

Finally Dylan reappears, his mother on his arm. His curls are slicked down with gel, his freckles evened out under make-up.

Pamela is dressed in a 1960s maxi dress in orange and brown. She looks terrific, and she knows it.

We shuffle along the corridor and take our places in the wings. There are lots of winks, and thumbs-up signs, and instructions to break a leg.

'God, I'm nervous,' whispers Serena.

None of us are able to keep still.

Standing in the opposite wings, Dylan's churchwarden waves at me. In return, I give him the nod to raise the curtain. Harry brings out a pocket flute and plays one long, soft note. We all try to hold it in our heads. As the velvet rises, the noises from the audience subside as they offer up to us their collective goodwill.

Dylan, as the lead character, Bobby, walks to the middle of the stage. He goes to his answer machine, hits 'play', and listens as our pre-recorded voices ring out with messages of friendship. Julian brings in the bass player, two violins, and plays some chords of his own on the piano. Then silence. Off stage, *a cappella* – using Harry's note – we start intoning Bobby's name in harmony, building to a crescendo of multi-part harmonies. Then, one by one, we join Dylan on stage. In my hands I carry the enormous cake. I feel alive. We are ready.

Chapter Thirty-three

E'N UNTO ETERNITY.

The restaurant surfaces are smooth and shiny. The sound of clinking glasses bounces off the black marble and chrome. The hands of our fellow diners flash with signet rings, or chunky jewels; there's a lot of hairspray in the air. I've scrutinised everybody. Matt and I are waiting for Dylan, who is forty minutes late. I twist my napkin into a tight coil and loop it round my finger. The waiter meets Matt's request for more olive bread.

'Stop worrying,' says Matt, reaching across the table to cover my hand.

'But suppose something's gone wrong. This could destroy him.'

Last month's dreaded meeting with the Bishop had an unexpected outcome. Far from heralding the end of Dylan's career, it had sparked a certain renaissance. Having refused to play the sacrificial lamb, he had found himself anointed a disciple. For it came to pass that the man and the office were at war. In public, the Bishop sided with the conservatives and emphasised church orthodoxy. Privately, he and his wife held more liberal views. It was time, he told Dylan, to throw off the chasuble of hypocrisy; to sweep away the age of 'Don't ask, don't tell', and usher in a new era of tolerance. Dylan had been appointed his spokesman, and today was his first engagement: to speak in a televised debate on gay adoption.

Who'd have thought it? Growing up, I planned things meticulously: I skipped in multiples of four, later tens; I avoided cracks on the pavement; I handed in my homework on time. In southern Africa, in the face of racial tension, poverty and crime, everyone has always talked of 'making a plan'. It means the opposite of how I lived; it means being spontaneous, going with the flow. Matt's motto is that life works out – but not necessarily in the way you expect.

'Thank God,' cries Matt, rising from his chair. 'It's the Pol Roger Padre!'

'Pol Rogers all round – my treasurer tells me we made nearly three thousand pounds with the show last week! My mother says it was her face on the posters that did it,' Dylan adds, sinking into his chair. 'Hey! You've gone brown,' he says, stroking my hair.

'Chestnut, please! It's my natural colour. Tell us about the debate,' I say, hurriedly. 'How did it go? We were so worried.'

'That's the royal "we", you understand,' grins Matt.

'Well, the gloves are off !' says Dylan, demanding a large gin and tonic. 'Today's the day we of the broad Anglican Church stood up to be counted.'

'Came out of the closet, you mean,' says Matt.

'Shouldn't you be at work?' says Dylan, scanning the menu.

'Oh, but I am,' laughs Matt. 'You're my Care in the Community project for today.'

'I'm flattered!' Dylan stretches and touches a waiter lightly on the arm. 'Excuse me. What's the soup today?'

'Radish and artichoke. Don't even go there.'

Dylan looks at us and pulls a face. 'Now – where was I?'

'You stood up to be counted,' I repeat.

'Ah, yes,' he says, breaking bread. 'We've had amazing publicity. And people on the street holding placards supporting gay clergy. Someone threw an egg, but it missed me.' Dylan pops a bread cube into his mouth. 'Nerve-racking, but exciting. It's probably a bit like discovering you're pregnant!' he laughs.

Matt and I steal a glance.

'But I'm doing my bit. And, God willing, it will be so e'n unto eternity—'

'Toad in the hole?' announces a waiter, with disdain.

*

Dylan and Matt suck on their cigars, exhaling long grey ghosts that tango over the table. My napkin is now a crumple of origami. A waiter deposits two small glasses of honey-coloured liquid before the men.

'Aren't you having one?' asks Dylan, surprised. I shake my head and reach out for my water glass. 'Oh, go on. It'll do you good.'

I look over at Matt and then back at Dylan.

'What? What am I missing?' says Dylan, propping his cigar in the groove of the ashtray.

'We've decided to adopt you,' laughs Matt. 'You're our errant teenage son.'

'I'm blessed. But seriously, what's with the … *No!*' Dylan stares at me. 'You're not—?'

I watch his cigar burn into wrinkles of ash, joined to the shaft by invisible threads.

'Let me tell you something, Dyl,' says Matt. 'Have you ever heard of Oudtshoorn?'

'No,' said Dylan.

'It's a place in the Western Cape famous for ostrich farming. My parents plan to retire there, which is rather appropriate. They're very traditional. Nationalist Party, not ANC. My father had the farm, my mother had me.' Matt takes a sip of dessert wine. 'Long ago, my mother's view of herself as a good mother withered and died, and she never got over it. She buried her head in the sand. I understand her, but I am not her. I chose a life, not just an existence.' He reaches out for my hand and squeezes it. 'Life is about loss. It knocks you down, and you find new ways of muddling through. You make choices.'

'Ah, but how do you know you've made the *right* choice?' says Dylan.

Matt smiles and shakes his head. 'You learn that sometimes there is no right choice. The important thing is to own the choices you make.'

'Don't tell me, after all this time, you've chosen to have a baby?' cries Dylan.

'Not as such,' I say, slowly.

Matt gets up and announces he's going to the bathroom.

'Damn,' says Dylan. 'He's gone for the bill. I know he's gone for the bill.'

'Forget it. You can get the bread and wine round yours next time.'

'But I don't understand,' Dylan groans. 'The message you left on my mobile this morning said you had something to tell me. If you're not pregnant, what is it?'

Around us, empty tables are being re-laid for the evening shift – crisp linen, sparkling glasses, set with precision. A waiter is aligning the knives just so. It reminds me of how as a child I couldn't go to sleep at night unless the bedroom door was pulled to at just the right angle.

I reach out for Dylan's hands, and he listens as I explain as fully as I can.

'Ah, my girls who gorge!' cries Matt, approaching our table carrying coats.

'Well, let me propose a toast,' roars Dylan, as he rises from the table, an imaginary glass in his hand. 'To our family of friends. And to tolerance!'

'I think we've just exceeded our limit here of both,' I say, laughing. And I steer Dylan by the elbow between the tables and out on to the pavement.

Epilogue

*D*O *YOU REPENT?*

Life is held together by ritual. From the very first pattern of four-hourly feeds, the human body instinctively responds favourably to routine. Ruptures to what is familiar can deal a seismic blow. Nursery rhymes, regular bath-times, favourite toys, all imbue a baby with a warm sense of containment, and love. The Christening is the first opportunity the Church has to demonstrate its own version of that love to an infant, paving the way for a lifetime of ritual and sanctuary.

'Good grief. Do you think Dylan wrote this rubbish?' whispers Harry, flapping his order of service under his wife's nose.

'Shhhh,' says Serena, reaching into her handbag to pass Harry the indigestion tablets she knows he needs.

Around the congregation, people lean forward. Dylan has dropped his voice now, and is addressing only the naked baby in his arms, who lies mesmerised by Dylan's deep, seductive tones, by words only he is privileged to hear. It's highly nuanced communication of the utmost intimacy. Osmotic. Where each picks up something unspoken from the other. And when Dylan lays the baby gently in the water in the font, the baby looks about him not with terror, but with recognition, that this lilting liquid is a place of safety, of glorious beginnings. And he lets out a gurgle of contentment, as though he has finally come home.

I repent.

Parents and godparents take turns to hold the baby, now flushed from his impromptu bath and wrapped in soft towelling. Together they make their vows, and repent of their sins, and declare their commitment to this new life. And, as Amber passes the softly wriggling bundle to her neighbour, she turns to take in the new alabaster statue of Mary (a gift from an anonymous – grateful, Episcopal – donor). She marvels at the fresh lustre to its paintwork, bathed now in the sunlight filtering through the triptych windows. She knows she has made the right decision.

And then it's back to Amber and Matt's for celebratory tea. Matt has persuaded her to hire in help, so students wander the rooms topping up glasses of champagne and passing round catered trays of miniature delicacies. She was sceptical, but lately even she has found that the soft dips and purées and sloppy risottos of what Dylan now dubs her toddler phase are being slowly replaced by recipes with a bit more bite.

Amber stands at the window of the marital bedroom. In the garden she watches Esme tugging Tallulah's tail. Far from escaping, or turning on the child in feline spite, the cat seems to relish the rough and tumble of the game. Harry is erecting a folding chair and, behind him, Nicole slouches, with her hands rubbing at her pelvis, before easing herself into it. Serena is talking to Dylan. Matt is showing Dominic how to tie up lavender plants for the winter, and Dominic even looks interested. Just then a thick yellow thatch comes into view as Piers steps through the French doors, holding William tightly in his arms. The baby is facing outward, distracted now by the beads of Eloise's necklace, jigging all four limbs at once, as though eager to get on with this business called life. Louisa appears, and prises William from the arms of her boyfriend. For this one moment, all Amber's friends are connected, framed by the window in a vivid canvas of glorious, everyday harmony.

'You, I love,' murmurs Amber. She's getting used to the idea of starting with 'you' and not 'I' – more like, she thinks, how love should be.

As Amber reaches the bottom of the stairs, she sees her holdall. Her heart misses a beat. She makes her way to the kitchen, and then the garden. She can almost sense the days shortening around her.

At her touch, Matt straightens and turns round. He asks Dominic to excuse him and follows his wife. Two girls wash baking sheets at the sink. A young man lifts complicated canapés from a plastic box on to glass plates decorated with berries.

'I'm terrified,' she whispers, as they climb the stairs together.

'I know,' he says, picking up the holdall and taking hold of her hand.

*

Eventually the remaining guests move on to coffee; they have abandoned the garden and are mingling in the drawing room. When Dylan tries to initiate a reprise of *Company* songs, he is rugby-tackled off the piano stool by Harry. William, from his vantage point on his grandmother's knees, finds the incident hilarious. Serena sinks down on the sofa next to Prue.

'Wasn't he good in the church today?' she murmurs, letting William clutch at her finger. 'Esme bit the vicar's finger when she was only five months old,' she adds, beaming.

'I'm so glad you were able to bring all the girls,' says Prue, bouncing William gently as she speaks. 'I don't know how we would've accommodated everyone if we'd held the party in Louisa's flat. There's only the small terrace, for a start – not like the garden here. I've bought Amber and Matt a photo frame to thank them for hosting the party. Do you think they'll like it? They seem to have enough already.' She accompanies this observation with a tilt of the head towards the piano, and its regiment of photo frames.

'Oh, Amber loves her photographs. You can be sure your present will be very welcome. Incidentally, where is she? Amber, I mean.' Serena heaves herself on her knuckles towards the edge of the sofa and looks around. 'And Matt. Dylan, where are Matt and Amber?' Dylan comes over. 'Where's our perfect hostess?' continues Serena. 'She never abandons us. This is weird,' she confides to Prue. 'Is something wrong?' she asks, looking back at Dylan.

'And don't start quoting *Company* to me!' Serena adds, giving Dylan a playful thump. 'I don't ever want to hear anything of that show ever again. Last month nearly finished me off !'

'But it was worth it, wasn't it?' says Prue, eyeing Dylan carefully, sensing the need to steer the conversation. 'I babysat for Louisa and Piers when they went to see you all in the show, and they said it was tremendous. Serena, they especially loved your scene with the chocolate brownie.'

Serena accepts the compliment. 'But it was exhausting. I lost pounds – in spite of all that cake! Maybe Amber's having a lie-down. Shall I go and see?' She makes to rise.

'She's not having a lie-down,' says Dylan.

'Who's not having a lie-down?' says Harry, approaching.

'Amber, Harry. And Matt.'

'And the significance of this startling piece of information is?'

'That they're not here,' wails Serena. 'Our hosts are not here. They've always been here for us, and now they're not.'

Harry turns to Dylan. 'Do you know anything about this?'

'William, I think it's past your bedtime,' says Prue, standing up abruptly with the baby cradled in the crook of one arm.

'I think it's time we went, too,' says Harry, alert to the sense, if not the specifics, of the situation. He extends an arm to his wife. 'Come on, girl. We're almost the last ones to leave.'

'But what about—?'

'Shhhh,' he says, smiling. 'I'll help you round up our brood.' They walk out of the room, hand in hand.

Dylan smiles at Prue, just as Louisa and Piers join them.

'I take it they've gone?' asks Piers.

Dylan nods. 'You recommended the clinic, I gather.'

'A friend of mine from medical school. A meticulous clinician. She's pioneering some new techniques. It was the least I could do.'

'Well, we mustn't get our hopes up too much—' says Dylan.

'But they do happen, don't they? Miracles I mean,' says Louisa, stroking the soft contours of her son's warm head.

Yes, they do, thinks Piers.

*

The night before, Amber dreamt that guests had met for the christening party, but that her kitchen cupboards were found to be empty, devoid of all provisions. Its meaning had seemed so transparent, that in the morning she had decided not to tell Matt. For what other interpretation could there be? Everyone had been relying on her, and once more she had let them down. Her planning had been deficient.

241

On into the drizzling twilight, as Matt drives her through winding suburban streets, and beyond to where the wooded Common fans out on either side of the road, she remains haunted by the dream. She asks Matt if they might change radio stations, to something inane and commercial. And so, by singing along and mocking the phone-ins on Robbie Taylor's show, she is able to hide her unease.

Soon the trees of the Common, as they are caught in the glare of the passing headlights, flash their barks of silver like protective shields, and seem to stand as heraldic guardians of an ideal, armed and ready to defend Amber's choice from all challengers. Occasionally through the branches she catches sight of a full moon, the colour of crème caramel.

And she knows now that there is never a right or wrong answer to the question of whether or not to have a baby. What matters is to remember to ask the question at all.

Eventually, the car scrunches along the gravel drive of the clinic and comes to a stop. A woman with vivid, geometric patterns on her jumper emerges from the main door. For an hour she has been anticipating the papal white smoke of these headlights in the November twilight.

'What are you doing here?' cries Amber, getting out of the car.

'I'll bring your case,' calls Matt through the open door, before pulling away in the direction of the car park.

'I don't know,' says Jenny. 'I mean, I wanted to see you, before you— To thank you—'

'You've thanked me hundreds of times!'

'No, but properly. I wanted to thank you by being here in person.' In unison, their shoes scrape on stone as they climb the steps. 'I felt so guilty—'

Amber hesitates in the doorway. 'Guilty?'

'This past month must have been a nightmare for you. You've had blood tests, and all sorts of gynae stuff.' Jenny wipes away tears with the cuff of her jumper.

'Not to mention all these wild new hormones raging around my system!' laughs Amber. 'But seriously,' she adds, 'don't feel guilty.' They walk towards the reception counter. 'This is my choice.'

After signing in, Amber and Jenny enter the waiting room, where Clive and Ginny are sitting on Cubist suede furniture. Clive rises, and bows his head. His face is grave, just as it was when they'd met a month ago to sign the necessary legal documents. The black hairs of his moustache are a line of exclamation marks. Amber knows she stands before a man stretched taut by vulnerability.

Amber kisses Ginny. 'Have they found you a room to work in?'

'Oh, yes,' Ginny laughs. 'They know me here of old. I've set up, so I'm ready when you are.' She turns to Jenny. 'If you like, I could give you a treatment after I've worked on Amber. Reflexology will help ease the stress and make you more receptive to tomorrow's implantation.'

'God, it's cold out there,' cries Matt, entering the waiting room. He warms his hands in his armpits. Amber instinctively moves to his side. She thinks of her impending sedation, and the complex spirals of DNA looped within her precious eggs.

The clinic's medical director enters the room and renews her acquaintance with each of them. Pleasantries are exchanged, and then she asks to speak to Amber alone.

As they mount a flight of graceful Georgian stairs, Amber strokes the waxed wood of the banister. It seems to her that she is accessing a celestial world, intoxicating in its atmosphere of heightened emotion. After a lifetime of confusion, this is no small consolation.

There is an irony, she can see now, in feeling at her most complete when part of her body is about to be removed for ever.

'Please. Take a seat,' says Dr Ramji, once they reach her tidy consulting room. 'I expect you're feeling rather nervous.'

Amber takes a chair opposite a polished desk. She nods, captivated by the woman's eyebrows: immaculate crescents of smooth, dark hairs along the line of the brow.

'I know you've signed all the papers and have met a few times with our counsellor. But it's my duty to have one last little chat. You are aware that this procedure may not work. You're at the upper age limit for donors, after all. I just want to confirm that, even at this late stage, you are fully committed. Are you ready to take the risk?'

*

Closing the front door, Dylan finds Tallulah circling his ankles. She rubs herself against him, using his shin as a loofah. 'Don't worry,' he says. 'They'll be back soon.' And he picks her up and carries her down to the kitchen. In the fridge they find an open can of food. The word 'Sunday' has been scratched on to the label in biro. After she eats the portion he scrapes out for her, he carries her upstairs to the drawing room, where he puts on a CD of a West End production of *Company*, and falls asleep to the familiar music. The cat nestles in his lap.

*

Amber is still not entirely certain what triggered her decision to donate her eggs to Jenny. When she was a child, she subscribed to the view that it was her role to keep her parents happy. That they were clearly miserable became for her not only a source of great imminent threat to her personal salvation, but a slur on her ability to function successfully. She sees now that such doubt in her own abilities was misplaced, a delusion based on inadequate information. It was never her duty to repair the damage of her mother's misfortunes. Perhaps egg donation is her last hurrah in making someone happy.

*

Ginny's view is that it is the universe itself, not God, which is mysterious. (Dylan pretends to be appalled, but he has rather fallen for Ginny. He has begun seeing her once a week. So far, his sinuses are clearer and his intolerance to cat fur has stopped, so he's prepared to indulge her in her primitive superstitions.) It is a simple view, and one with which Amber agrees. The alternative theory – that the world is logical and that all future disappointments can be eliminated by advanced planning – has been proved of late to be somewhat outdated.

*

Before replying to the doctor, Amber sits for a moment in thought. New life, she considers, does not begin with birth. It extends further back than even conception. We are so much a product of what has gone before. So it is with rebirth. We cannot eliminate our history but can learn to accept it, tolerate it even, and integrate it into our new being. Like a painting, she thinks, painted over an existing one on the same piece of canvas. The old paint still exists, giving depth to the new.

I don't know, she suddenly wants to ask Dr Ramji, *if you ever catch Robbie Taylor on London Talks radio*. Because in her mind Amber has so much she wants to say, by way of explanation. There is always the choice to do things differently.

But she stops herself. Maybe there has been sufficient analysis, sufficient interpretation.

Instead she finds herself smiling spontaneously.

'I'm ready,' she says. 'I'm ready now.'

Acknowledgements

I would like to thank the following people:
Virginia Whetter, for her care, wisdom, and the occasional timely kick up the backside; Tai Long, for knowing something about absolutely bloody everything, and for teaching me to breathe; Paul McWilliam, for more dinner discussions about writing and publishing than a good friend should have to endure; Jeremy Vine, for motivational pep talks when the going seemed too tough – oh yeah, and the small matter of the title.

I also wish to thank:
Jill Robinson, & the Thursday night Wimpole Street Writers, for good food and feedback; Harry Bingham, Tricia Wastvedt, and Ashley Stokes at the Writers' Workshop for their perceptive criticism and guidance; Radhi and Vikram Mathur, for help with the finer points of Delhi slang; Jane Livesey, for long conversations on topics central to this novel; Christopher Eyden, Joseph Hawes and Piers Northam, for matters religious (AMDG!); Peter Bezuidenhoudt, for help with South African history; Laurel Remington, for heroic eleventh hour insights.

Special thanks to:
All at Duckworth, especially Caroline McArthur and Suzannah Rich, for making it happen; Michael Alcock, my agent, for his steady hand, for loving this book, and for shedding that tear.

But above all, to my husband Guy, whose precious presence in my life is both humbling and inspiring: thank you for finding me.

In memory of Christian Robertet, who made me promise
never to give up on my dreams

Life is nothing without friendship